The Hoax

Nikki Rodwell

Published by **Nixie Books**

Cover design by **Nikki Rodwell**

The Hoax © 2023 **Nikki Rodwell**

The Hoax

www.nikkirodwell.co.uk

ISBN: 9781916398931 (paperback)

Table of Contents

Free exclusive content for readers of 'The Hoax'

https://bit.ly/the-hoax

The fool doth think he is wise, but the wise man knows himself to be a fool.

William Shakespeare

PROLOGUE

The room is stifling, thick with cigar smoke hanging under the dim overhead light like a canopy. The dark corners of the room seem to close in as the other players lean forward to watch with bated breath. I slide the last of my evening's winnings forward, making the pile on the table look like a bunch of paper Monopoly money. My total gamble stands at thirty grand now, and I know my opponent can't match it. The river card has been dealt and this is the end.

"All in," I say.

Jeremy lets out a small gasp – I know he thinks I'm bluffing again. He knows me better than anyone else around the table, but he's never seen me double bluff like this. His eyes widen as he waits for the reaction, fiddling with the corners of the cards he is about to deal.

Jeremy is the one who invited us all here tonight, but I don't think he ever intended for things to spiral quite so out of control. Bets are unlimited, and the other players folded in our last round, sensing the stand-off between me and the big guy sitting opposite me. His face is pitted with acne scars, and he looks like some big sugar daddy as he puffs on his cigar, his young piece of crumpet hanging off his arm. Pete, I think they called him. I've never met the man before tonight, and something tells me I don't ever want to meet him again. There's something a little unnerving about him, almost mafia-like.

He leans back in his chair, watching me. His fingers are almost as thick as the cigar he holds between his index and middle finger, and he takes a long drag before puffing out a billow of smoke as if it stung the insides of his mouth. I maintain eye contact, ensuring my jaw is clamped and my face is neutral. I don't want to give him a hint of emotion. My stomach is doing somersaults, but I visualise the sensation as a compressible gas fizzing in my stomach. I bottle it before it can rise through my system, affecting my heartrate or body temperature.

As we eyeball each other, two tiny creases mark his brow, revealing his frustration. A bead of sweat trickles down his forehead. He can't match my bet and I know that he's cornered.

The woman, presumably his fiancée judging by the rock on her wedding finger, leans in and whispers something in his ear. She's like one of those trophy wives you see attached to the arms of famous footballers, all silicon and fake smiles. I don't know what she's doing here tonight; these events usually happen in the backroom or basements of the men's club, which aren't the place for a woman. But tonight, being as we're in Jeremy's pad, she was allowed in for some reason.

The den is Jeremy's man cave. The room is set out like a cinema, with a seventy-inch TV with the latest tech surround speakers at one end. The six black leather recliner chairs are positioned for prime viewing in a semi-circle around the TV in front of a smoked glass coffee table which is scattered with an array of remote controls, barely visible since that end of the room is unlit.

We're seated in the other half of the room, around a mahogany Regency-style table. Its craftsmanship would be the envy of any home card player. The round centre has a tactile brown leather playing surface, and each of us has an ornate brass chip holder which we use as ashtrays since we play with cash. It's a sacrilege to the intended purpose, but they are routinely removed and polished up to be replaced for future games.

The drinks cabinet on the wall behind my opponent is a mess; the Tiffany lamp highlights the surface strewn with glasses and half-drunk bottles of whisky and red wine. My crystal tumbler still contains a healthy measure of single malt whisky, which I take a sip of as I wait for his next move.

The other players hover, obviously itching to leave, but equally unable to tear themselves away before seeing the outcome between my opponent and me. There is no attempt to reach in his pocket for any hidden cash. Clearly, I have wrung him dry, and other than throwing his car keys into the mix – which has been known in the past – the party is over for him.

The blonde-haired bimbo fiddles with something on her wrist and leans in to whisper in his ear again. He nods, and she removes a bracelet which she presents to him submissively. He takes the sparkly piece from her and tosses it onto the leather table. The pile of notes softens its landing.

At first, I think it's a snake of some kind, the head is almost like that of a reptile with stone eyes, but then I realise the diamond-encrusted circle evolves into the head of a panther, its green emerald eyes challenging me.

"Genuine Cartier bracelet, I raise your bid by another 50K," he says.

"You can't raise with that, Pete," Mike says, looking at the others for approval.

There are frantic whispers and a sense of unrest between everyone.

"It's my call," says Jeremy. "As host of the evening, and current dealer, I get to arbitrate. If Ronnie is happy to play, then play – but all in."

"I accept," I say. His attempt to raise me has failed, but we're even now.

My heart is pounding; he must have a good hand, and I know he thinks I'm bluffing, but unless he has a royal flush, I've got this in the bag.

He stubs out his cigar in the thick glass ashtray which is provided for cigar smokers. The ash spills over the sides in his clumsy attempt to disguise his nerves. He places his cards face up onto the table, his eyes firmly fixed to mine. I glance down, barely taking a breath. The cards reveal four proud Jacks, and Pete looks smug.

I lean towards the table and slowly place down my cards, revealing a flush. The run of red diamonds are triumphant, and with the flick of a switch, the tension is released. Everyone congratulates me and takes a final swig of their drink, patting me on the back as they prepare to leave. I can feel Jeremy's relief as he sweeps the pile of cash and bracelet across to my side of the table. He clearly wanted me to see this Pete guy off, and my mission has been successfully accomplished.

"Let's wrap this up, gentlemen, it's late, and the missus will have my guts for garters if I don't get this place cleaned up before the morning," Jeremy says.

Pete and his fiancée give each other a sideways glance, before standing up from the table. She grabs her fur coat from the back of her chair, and, without so much as a goodwill handshake or glance in my direction, they swiftly head towards the door, making their silent exit. They're clearly crushed by their loss. But all's fair in love and war, and I won that fair and square. It could have gone either way, but the odds were on my side tonight.

Nobody comments on the abrupt exit, or the lack of politeness. I grab my jacket from the back of my chair, and after thanking Jeremy and shaking everyone's hand, I make my way to the cab waiting outside.

As we travel through the empty leafy streets, the taxi driver hums to himself, leaving me to my thoughts of how I'll hide tonight's winnings from Amanda. I've promised my wife that I've given up my poker evenings, but this game was special; a one-off. I told her that me and the lads were having a film night and that she wasn't to wait up, as knowing Jeremy, he wouldn't be able to decide what to watch so we would probably end up watching at least two gangster movies.

I rub my jacket pocket, feeling the hard round bulge of the bracelet that has just come into my possession. I'll probably take it to Emcy's and get it valued, but then I'll sit on it a while and decide what to do with it. I know I can't give it to Amanda.

I'm a man of my word, and as I watch the glow of the streetlamps streaking past, I think that possibly tonight is the right time to knock these games on the head for good. The buzz I feel is a mix of alcohol and the delightful sensation of success. It's always best to quit while you're ahead.

Chapter 1

RONNIE

It's a snug fit as I pull the Aston into the space marked for 'Chairman'. Two company Mercedes are annoyingly close on either side. I can't really complain though since I'm more of a non-executive CEO these days.

Ever since 'Back Up' went public in 2004, I have semi-retired, leaving Martyn as managing director and running the whole show. He's been with me since I began the business back in 1990 and I trust him with my baby – wouldn't trust him with my car though.

I nudge up towards the wall until the continuous beep sounds, and then turn off the engine, leaving an empty void in place of the beefy growl that had previously bounced off the walls in the underground car park.

I'm late. Not my fault, the traffic was hellish. No doubt I'll get a dressing down from our company secretary Penny since we only have these board meetings a couple of times a year, and they're the only thing that pulls me back into the office these days. Penny hates me being late, but I like the banter with her in the office, especially when she pretends to be cross with me – when she gives me that look of hers which says, 'You're late, Mr Taylor'. It turns me on, if I'm honest, her puppy dog eyes flirting with me, whilst her attempt at being strict just makes me think of her in stockings and suspenders.

I press the top button in the lift and straighten my jacket and tie, glancing at my reflection in the mirror. My hair is looking grey – far too many silver highlights for my liking. Shit! Where did the time go? Women say grey hair makes a man look more distinguished but at forty-five it makes me scarily aware that middle age has arrived, and I don't want to get old. I have so much to do yet.

Amanda and I want to travel, explore parts of the world we haven't yet seen, and I have other projects up my sleeve too. The thing about money, I've discovered, is that no matter how much you make, you always want to make more. It's addictive. They say 'money doesn't bring happiness', well my reply to that is, 'better to be rich and miserable than poor and miserable', and besides, it quenches my insatiable desire for success.

I'm more than grateful for being in the luxurious position of owning a multi-million-pound business, but I'm beginning to realise that reaching my pinnacle with this little empire has now left a bit of a void. The real fun – the excitement – was in the making of it. In the early days I was run ragged, convincing businesses that my idea of a rope escape ladder fixed to windowsills was a necessity, not a luxury. Such a simple little invention but one that saves lives and gives peace of mind, even to domestic homeowners – although there *were* some complaints when their wretched teenagers decided to use it to escape from their bedrooms for a night on the tiles. But I'm a man who likes competition, I thrive on challenges and a small part of me misses the pull that drove me to make this business the success it is, but that impetus has been handed over to Martyn now.

The lift doors open, and I stride towards the boardroom, barely taking in the floor of staff who are beavering away at their desks with phones glued to their ears. I don't know any of the workers here anymore; I'm not involved in the daily running, and leave Charles our HR manager to take care of the staffing side of things. I have to say it's far tougher for him than it was in my day.

Martyn and I only had a team of around fifty, and we didn't have all the red tape and regulations that restrict everything these days. You can't fire people the way I used to, especially if they're of a minority ethnic group or homosexual. We used to be able to ask a woman at interview if she planned to have a baby, and yes, if she were young and recently married, I wouldn't waste my time by giving her the job. But that's all changed now. This is the twenty-first century, as Martyn is always reminding me.

Penny sees me through the boardroom window and rushes out to greet me with the agenda and documents I need for the meeting. She shoves them in my hand.

"You're late." Her eyes widen to warn me that I'm in trouble, but I just smile.

3

"Black with one sugar, please, hon," I say, before sweeping into the boardroom and taking my place in the soft leather executive chair at the top end of the table.

It's like a G7 conference, only twice the size. The directors are all wearing their Armani suits and silk ties, with their Mont Blanc pens at the ready.

I acknowledge my chief in command, Martyn Skinner, whom I have a love-hate relationship with. Love, on the tennis court, where I can still knock him into shape, and hate, when we lock horns with ways forward with the company. Whilst I respect that he runs the company well, I can't help but point out when I think he's getting it wrong. He's not a risk taker like me, and you can't expect to have big results without taking the odd risk. I'm not so sure he's such a good judge of character as me either, he's far too trusting. It pained me to have to tell him 'I told you so' when our last chief finance officer turned out to be as bent as a nine-bob note. But just like children, sometimes people need to learn lessons the hard way.

"Morning, Ronnie… or is it afternoon?" Martyn says, raising a chuckle in the room.

"Morning, Skinner, tell me, are you looking thinner?" It's a long-standing joke of ours since he is quite overweight and forever trying some new-fangled diet.

"I hope you don't mind, but we made a start without you," says Bob, our rather anaemic-looking chief accountant, who always looks incredibly nervous when I'm around.

4

"Not at all," I reply. "I'm only here for the fun bit; shall we get straight to it and discuss the school proposal for Back Up Security?"

I've seen the figures that have been quoted after a recent bid for a group of independent schools. Whilst offering CCTV and top spec camera systems and alarms to the public domain is a more recent venture, I don't believe we're doing ourselves any favours by turning down the offer. Our escape ladders have been remodelled and sold to so many other manufacturers, it takes care of itself these days. Our sister company that deals with the security element is largely hitting the domestic market, but if we're to get the same success that we have had with Back Up Escape, it's crucial we get away from domestic use and dig deeper into the public sector.

"But we're undervaluing ourselves." Simon is the first to pipe up with his protest. He's our marketing director who works closely with the tech team. "Our range is unbeatable for its infrared technology, and we even have an app now for managing the system remotely."

Yes, Martyn did mention something about an app when we last played tennis, but I was three games down in the final set and didn't pay much attention.

"I don't care if it's bloody solar-powered and teaches the kids their algebra! If we take the contract, we prove ourselves in the education field," I say, nodding at Penny as she places a gold-rimmed china cup of steaming black coffee in front of me.

I watch her walk back to her seat, taking in the shape of her in her tight pencil skirt with her slender calves shaded in what I imagine to be stockings. Her high-heeled glossy shoes give her a sexy wiggle and I feel myself already wishing this meeting were over. I must wangle a way to make sure it's over by lunchtime if I'm to have time to go back to hers during her lunch hour.

I know I come across as a tad arrogant in the boardroom, but this is my comfort zone. I've learnt this business inside out from the ground up over the last twenty-five years. I know what works, and I know what doesn't. Although, as Martyn keeps reminding me 'times have changed since your day' and the changes in technology have brought different obstacles. But, I'm old-school, even down to the leather Filofax I have in my briefcase. I don't trust a mobile to keep all my dates and figures safe; I'd far rather see ink on paper than think of my life being held by some filing system up in the cloud.

I flick open the gold clasps on my black briefcase and remove my faithful friend, glancing at the bevelled metal object tucked in the corner of my case before shutting it again.

Penny scribbles away on her notepad. I love the fact that she's old-school, like me; she jots every word down in shorthand. It can't be easy for her to keep up, since the heated discussion that follows is thrown around the table like a hot potato, everyone vying for their point of view to be heard and wanting the final say. Their need to be right, to 'win' across the table, amuses me. There are those that like to antagonise, purely for the sake of it, constantly contradicting what was said before. Then there are others that are too scared to throw their opinions on the table for fear of not going with the majority.

I suddenly get the urge. Not of the sexual kind, but more of a psychological compulsion that creeps over me sometimes. It often rears its head at the most inappropriate times, taunting me until the schoolboy rises to the surface. It is like some devil constantly perches on my shoulder, biding its time until it nudges me to play again.

I love practical jokes, not so much for attention, but rather to see the look on people's faces in that one moment of blissful confusion. I think it stems from watching too many episodes of *Beadle's About* where the host plays elaborate jokes on his victims, catching them unawares and recording their reactions. The fact that so many millions of viewers tuned in to watch it during the nineties is proof that people love a good joke. It's human nature to laugh at somebody else's misfortune, and the person who's the brunt of it has that wonderful moment of release when the joke is revealed. It's a bit like a punchline with props.

I lean forwards and flip open the two gold clasps on my briefcase again. The leather creaks as the case expands open with the front panel fully shielding its contents from view.

I sense faces looking in my direction as the discussion pauses. I stand up and carefully remove the gunmetal grenade from the corner of the case, its slightly worn metal surface a heavy weight in my hand.

With the case closed, it takes a few seconds for the party to register. Now, I know this is an old one, and I'm aware that Martyn has grown tired of this particular prank, but I've not done it in the office before. If just one person around this table has that moment of uncertainty, feels their heart pulsate with panic, then it's worth it.

I hold the grenade in front of me, placing my left hand on the pin, as if ready to remove it. The silence is deafening.

"What the –"

I interrupt Simon. "So, if we can't reach some agreement, I vote we give it to the dogs and let someone else start this business again from scratch."

The confused look on Simon's face gets the adrenaline flowing through my veins.

"We may as well scrap Back Up Security and go back to the way things were."

Penny drops her pencil and glares at me, searching for answers that she cannot find right now. I forgot she's never seen this, since the grenade usually lives on my coffee table at home.

The clock ticks on the wall, and the distant noise of traffic hums gently. I slowly pull the pin, holding the handle down securely and then place the pin on the table.

"R… Ronnie, what the hell's going on here?" Stephen, our operations director, has gone deathly pale, slowly leaning backwards into his chair as if he wants to curl himself into a tight ball. Martyn is giving me a look of distaste, his raised eyebrows telling me he's not amused. Julian, executive sales director, has obviously seen one of these before and rolls his eyeballs, but I ignore him.

My fingers slowly release the handle and… click. A flicker of light emerges as the flame of my lighter ignites.

"Anyone for a cigarette?" I ask, taking a packet of Marlboro from my back pocket.

The relief spreads around the room, Stephen suddenly laughing as if he knew all along it was one of my jokes. Penny disappears from the room to fetch me an ashtray.

"You bloody dickhead!" Martyn says, with a wide grin spreading across his face. He loved it really. I had two or three of them in the palm of my hand for that split second.

"You can't smoke that thing in here. Take it out on the smoker's balcony," he says.

The secret to a good joke is in the acting. My poker face and calmness has had years of practice, and I love that moment where the world seems to stop for a split second, looking at me to see if I'm kidding or not. It's childish, I know, but then it stems from childhood and what was once a necessity, as opposed to a frivolous pastime.

I was packed off to boarding school at the age of ten and the bullying that took place there was awful. I still can't pee in the toilet today, without recalling the time I was forced by sixth-formers to pee in a glass jug, and then drink it. The threat of being beaten up, or worse still, having them do the kind of shit they did to the other boys, was enough to make me do what they asked. The smell of urine made me gag repeatedly, and I vomited the moment they left my room.

There were other forfeits too, such as having to walk along the high plank in the gymnasium, with hockey balls and books being thrown at me to try and make me fall, and fagging: I would run continual errands or do chores to fulfil the older boys' power-driven demands.

I guess you could say my entrepreneurial side first made its appearance while I was still at school too. After many failed attempts at running away, and being told 'boarding school is character-building' or 'to man-up' by my father, I learnt ways to keep myself under the radar with the sixth-formers.

As I progressed to senior school, I would still run errands or give up my tuck box to the bullies, but thankfully I only experienced one episode of being roughed-up where I sustained an injury. I was clobbered in the face with a hockey stick which caused my lip to swell and one of my teeth to crack – it hurt like hell. There were also a few other bruises from being manhandled and shoved around in corridors. But, by comparison to the other boys in my year, I was let off lightly.

Rumours spread that the housemaster in one of the other boarding houses visited the boys after lights out, but thankfully I was spared from this harassment. The teachers knew what was going on but chose to ignore it; they probably thought it was all 'character-building' too.

One morning, I was woken up at five when Toby, the leader of the sixth-form gang, and his sidekicks thought it would be funny to position a small wooden table from our dorm over Edward Ecclestone's head. The poor boy was dead to the world and totally unaware that the ceiling had closed in on him, when he was rudely awoken by the sound of his alarm clock going off in his ear. He surfaced as if receiving an electric shock and sprang bolt upright, hitting his head smack bang on the dark wood just above his face. The bruise took weeks to fade. But it was then, as I peered from beneath my stiff white sheets, that I realised how the prefects enjoyed the thrill of their pranks more than they did raping or beating up the boys. It was all a display of their power and control, but even more so, the humiliation of their victims.

The next time I was cornered by Toby and co for another head dunking down the toilet, I pleaded my case.

"Look, I have a great idea that I think you'll be interested in."

"What could we possibly be interested in from *you*?" Toby said, his eyes screwed up and the bumfluff on his top lip forming a crooked line.

"Your pranks on the others has given me an idea," I said. "I've been reading up on practical jokes, and on my last visit home, I went to the joke shop and bought a few things. I've got some itching powder and fake bugs, and plenty of other ideas like food colouring that we can put in the showerhead. We could offer a service to the boys in my year and play practical jokes on their enemies, or even on the teachers, and get them to pay for it!"

Toby looked at the other two boys, and I sensed I might have just saved myself from getting my hair washed down the toilet.

"How would we get them to pay?"

"Well, we charge, say fifty pence per joke, which I'll carry out. I'll tell them that if anyone snitches, you guys will pay them a visit – that should keep them quiet. Then anyone who doesn't pay up, you can go and collect the debt?"

"And how do we split the money?"

"You three split it between you, and my payment is immunity from any more harassment from you."

Toby's eyebrows raised as his steely eyes bored into me.

"If it works, and you like my jokes, then so long as I keep them going and the money coming in, you agree to extend your immunity to all the boarders in my year."

There were ten of us boarding in my year, split into two rooms of five, but there were nearly a hundred boarders in total – plenty of others for them to prey on.

I knew that a lot of the overprivileged boys in my year received around twenty pounds per week pocket money as opposed to my meagre five pounds. They wouldn't think twice at giving up fifty pence, and even if only half the year took part, that would bring in around twenty pounds per joke.

"Eighty pence per student and you have a deal," Toby said, nodding at the others.

"Okay, I'll give it a go." I was already planning in my head to charge one pound to those who boasted how wealthy their families were, and pocket the difference.

Toby released my collar and shoved me towards the basins. "You've got a deal. First payment due by next Friday evening."

And that's how it began.

Payments were sparse to begin with, but as my popularity grew and the boys relished my pranks, I started to get more requests. Itching powder was sprinkled in PE tops, bugs strategically placed in toilet bags or beds, and I even sold packets of gum that I had replaced with flattened Blu Tack and rewrapped for an extra fifty pence.

The jokes that made the most profit were the ones on teachers, as the whole class would have to cough up the funds. A durex filled with custard was carefully positioned on the roller blackboard to make its appearance during Mr Griffin's French class; I would jump the lunch queue to lick a couple of dessert spoons laid out on the teacher's table before sprinkling them with pepper or salt, and my pièce de resistance was placing a perfectly-sized apple in the exhaust pipe of the deputy head's MGB, which sounded like a WWI cannon when it spectacularly fired. There wasn't a window on the east side of the school that wasn't filled with excited boys stifling their giggles.

I was lucky to get away with things as long as I did. There were numerous announcements made by the headmaster demanding that the school prankster be identified, but nobody ever dobbed me in and my cover was safe. Until my 0-level year.

A new set of sixth-form bullies had taken over from Toby and co who had left the previous year, and I stupidly took up a dare to switch the head boy's bottle of Coca-Cola for something a little more unpalatable. He caught me red-handed in the prefect room after switching his coke for lemonade just as I was pouring in some soy sauce to darken its colour. He grabbed me roughly by the arm and marched me to the head's office.

Of course, I denied all the other practical jokes that the head wanted answers for, and thank God, he was totally unaware of the double-dealing that had been going on. But the longshot was, I was encouraged to leave once my exams had finished and find an alternative college for sixth-form studies.

My parents were, of course, totally humiliated by my antics, and rather than 'wasting any more hard-earned money on me', I was sent to a state sixth form college. Why they always insisted on pretending they struggled to pay for my education was beyond me, since I knew it was my granddad's legacy that had paid the school fees.

So, despite leaving school at sixteen and never facing bullies again, I suppose some things stick, and for me, practical jokes became the norm.

My wife says I overstep the mark sometimes, but I'm not cruel. Take this situation, for example; it was only a matter of seconds before I showed the joke for what it was, revealing that the grenade was nothing more than just a cigarette lighter. It was just long enough to jolt their senses but not long enough for someone to go into a complete panic and beg me for mercy.

I leave the boardroom to go and stand on the 'naughty balcony' – the place where us lepers can smoke. What happened to the days when smoking wasn't such a crime? You could have that precious after-dinner cigarette at the restaurant table rather than standing out in the cold and rain like some bloody idiot. You could smoke on airplanes if you sat at the back, or (as in my case), up in first class. Surely if you pay enough for first-class treatment, they should allow you somewhere to smoke?

I return to the boardroom where I know I've been the subject of conversation. Penny has left me a fresh cup of coffee and I retake my place at the head of the table.

After further discussion on the school contract, we finally decide to take a vote. I'm relieved when the results show a 50/50 split which means I get the casting vote, so we settle on taking the contract.

The meeting is wrapped up, and a few colleagues are clearly disgruntled as they leave the boardroom, saying goodbye to me with steely faces as they head off back to their desks. I remain behind with Martyn and Charles, our HR manager.

"How's the new car?" Martyn asks.

"She's a beast," I reply. "Saw off a Porsche 911 at the lights on the way here."

Now, I wouldn't call myself an ostentatious man, I'm not like Martyn who enjoys being 'spoilt' with his chauffeur-driven Bentley and houses in every country for every season. You can smell his wealth a mile off, from his Bulgari cigarette lighter to the diamonds that drip off his wife, Meghan. But I *do* like my nice cars. It probably stems from my love of Scalextric as a child, but speed excites me, the feeling of all that power under the bonnet with my hands gripping the leather wheel.

"So, you want to discuss James?" Charles asks.

Penny pops her head around the door. "Will you gentlemen be requiring any lunch?"

"No thanks, Penny, we should only be half an hour, then I'll be heading off," I reply. I see the wry smile that curves those plump red lips, as she now knows what my lunchtime plans are.

"Martyn says you're proposing we put James into our Woking office. How will that work?" Charles asks.

My son James has worked for us for nearly two years now, and more than proved his worth. I didn't want him coming in with any special favours as the boss's son, he needs to earn respect.

When he first announced he wanted to come and join the firm, I was delighted, of course. I would love for him to take the full reins of the company one day, and whilst I don't like to mix family and business, he and I have a great relationship and it works.

His education has obviously paid off, and he's a quick learner. He first learnt the ropes by travelling the country and shadowing the sales reps, pricing up jobs, and even learning how to install our systems. But it wasn't long before he worked his way up in sales, and he clearly has the gift of the gab. He never fails to sell the full shebang to the innocent customer who only intended to buy a basic little motion detector. They end up with smart video doorbells, voice-activated room sensors and Wi-Fi cameras both inside and out. He's a chip off the old block.

"He's settling down now, and it's time to challenge him more," I say, the truth being he *is* settling down, with his new girlfriend Rachel. He asked me for an advance a few weeks back, to buy an engagement ring for her, and I'm hoping this will mean they will move in together a bit closer to home. Amanda and I live in what's known as the Golden Triangle of Surrey, a leafy suburb in Elmbridge supposedly dotted with celebrities. We would both love for them to live close by, so that we can play an active part in their lives and see our grandchildren, should we get them one day.

"I'm proposing he takes on more of a managerial role; more responsibility. Let's make him Sales & Marketing Manager for the southeast, he can oversee the others, put on training seminars and get involved in the strategic planning," I say matter-of-factly.

It's a foregone conclusion, and they both know it. There was little point in having this discussion really, since they know what I say, goes.

"That's a fantastic idea, Ronnie, but he'll have to wait until I find a replacement for him. I'll get onto it," Charles says.

Meeting over, we chat a while about our home life. Charles has just won some title with his golf endeavours – how he finds time to stroll around a golf-course, I don't know. Boring game if you ask me. His family are all doing well, and I feel a tinge of envy when he talks about his daughter who is heading off to university. Part of me would have loved a girl, 'Daddy's little girl' and all that. But Amanda was insistent she only wanted one child, even with my offer of a nanny to help her. So, I count my blessings. Whilst I was away a lot with business in the early years, James and I have had a lot of fun together over the years. Skiing trips, trips to the Grand Prix, tennis, and of course, plenty of practical jokes along the way.

"See you Saturday morning on court then," Martyn says, as we part company by the lift.

"Yep, and don't forget the winner pays for lunch," I reply, as the doors close.

Tennis is my sport. Martyn comes over every Saturday morning, weather permitting, and we play at mine. I have a mean competitive streak, and hate to lose. I've recently invested in some private coaching to work on my backhand and footwork since Martyn has won a little too often this last year, and seems to have found my Achilles heel. I haven't told him, of course, knowing that he would match my efforts and find himself a private coach too.

In the summer, when it's hot enough, Martyn's wife Meghan sometimes joins him, and she and the children use our pool. Amanda sometimes joins too, if she can bear to pull herself away from her beloved horses.

Amanda and I live in a five-bed period house set in three quarters of an acre with an outdoor swimming pool and my esteemed tennis court. It may sound like a home akin to Southfork, from Dallas, when I add that we have our own paddock and stables, but it's not. We're not in the realm of your five-million-pound properties on St George's Hill in Weybridge, where the likes of Martyn and his wife Meg live. All that wasted space would annoy me, and being ostentatious for the sake of it really grates on me. It stems from hearing my parents boasting to the world how their son was at a private boarding school; I swore that I would never be as pretentious or boastful as them.

Our home is fairly modest with the perfect size garden for our amenities, and has a double gate at the far end that opens onto an extra plot which I purchased to build Amanda's stables. I would suppose this adds another quarter of a million to the market price, but it's worth every penny since she's happy. So long as she's out in nature with the dogs and horses, bossing her stablehands around and giving private lessons on the new pony she's just acquired, she's sweet. It's a world apart from mine, I've never understood the creatures. Scared of them, if I'm honest.

The one time I ventured over to the stables, Amanda was getting Starlight tacked up for a ride; he's her big black beast, which she often tells me has more horsepower than my Aston could ever have. I don't deny he's a magnificent-looking animal; his thick neck and muscular torso would take any human years at the gym to achieve. He's an Arabian, which supposedly is one of the most loyal and intelligent breeds. But the bloody thing kicked me, which wasn't a sign of intelligence in my opinion. It took the wind out of me, and whilst Amanda made excuses, I'm not really interested. Too unpredictable for my liking, and my only memory of ever sitting on a horse brings tears to my eyes with the thought of my nuts being squashed on the saddle. No, the equestrian life is not for me.

I exit the underground car park and sunshine streams through the windscreen as I fasten my seatbelt. With the thought of Amanda out on a ride, wearing her navy-blue fleece and gilet, enjoying the last of the autumn sunshine, my guilt lessens.

The Aston roars as I head off towards Penny's, which is a five-minute drive from the office. Being as her desk was empty when I walked past, I've no doubt she's already slipping into something a little more comfortable for our lunchtime rendezvous.

Chapter 2

JAMES

I'm not very good at expressing myself. That's why I found it so difficult to propose to Rachel.

I know she's the one. We get on so well and have the same likes and dislikes in most things in life. She's a couple of years older than me, and is content with a quiet life – which suits me just fine. I may sound old beyond my twenty-two years, but a night in front of the TV with a takeaway, or a quiz night down at our local with a few friends is what I enjoy the most. It feels relaxed, no pressure to be something I'm not; it feels safe.

Dad thinks he's the first to know I'm asking Rachel to marry me, but I planned it that way so that he wouldn't be involved in the proposal. It would be just like him to spy on us and pounce out of a bush dressed as a news reporter and start flashing his camera. No, I needed my privacy, so I have already proposed, with the ring to come in a week or so.

I'm not a man's man like Dad, in fact I'm a woman's man but not in a womaniser kind of way. I find it easier to talk to women and have more female friends than I do male, which Dad has never understood. He thinks women are useful for two things, domestic chores or fulfilling his sexual needs. He would deny it, but I think he's quite misogynistic. I'll never forget when he surprised me with a strippergram on my eighteenth birthday.

We were in the local pub, with me having my first legal drink. Ray and Dad were there (Ray is Dad's best mate), and I'd invited a couple of friends from college, including Helena. She and I had become friends during the last year of college and Dad kept insisting we were an item, when we weren't. He couldn't get his head around the fact that I liked her as a friend and had no intention of sleeping with her – which had to mean I was gay.

Helena was the one who sensed my embarrassment when some random woman appeared out of nowhere, to start stripping off her police outfit to 'Sledgehammer' blasting from a portable stereo whilst shoving her cleavage in my face. Dad and Ray were laughing and cheering in their blokey manner, and I was forced to go along with it, but every inch of me wanted it over as quickly as possible.

My guard was let down, and I clearly failed in hiding my discomfort, since Helena said she felt so sorry for me afterwards. But I did my best to play along; Dad would have been furious if I hadn't shown some gratitude for his 'surprise'.

So, Dad was beyond delighted when I told him that Rachel and I are to be married. He was my age when he married Mum, and I cringed when he thumped me on the back, saying, "Like father, like son."

The proposal had been on my mind for some time, and I decided that one of our walks with our family dog Max would be the perfect moment. Max has been my companion for most of my childhood and he's getting old. Fourteen is a good age for a German Shepherd, and he has filled the void of both brother and sister in my life. He has shared the good and the bad times, but it's especially the difficult times when I've needed him the most, crying many tears into his long golden fur.

Rachel and I picked him up from Mum on a sunny Saturday morning and went to the local park for a stroll. Knowing how his hips are, and at Mum's insistence, we kept him on a lead and walked towards the duck pond to sit on a bench and take in the view. There was a chill in the air and Rachel wore her quilted Barbour jacket that I love her in. Her hair was loose, and she wore that contagious smile of hers that lights me up inside.

We sat chatting and my eyes were fixed to the sparkly mini capsule that I had fitted to Max's collar when I got him out of the boot of my car. Rachel still hadn't noticed it, despite it being bright pink and glaringly out of place against Max's tartan red collar.

"I love this time of year," Rachel said. "The way the sun shimmers on everything, and the orange and browns of all the fallen leaves, it makes me think of pumpkins and fireworks."

"And cuddling up together in front of a fire."

24

"But neither of us have got a fire." Her face glowed with the reflection of all the golden hues around us.

"We will, when we live together," I said, but we'd had many conversations about this, and Rachel was adamant that there was no rush, that her parents would only approve if she were to be committed in her relationship – preferably married.

Well, that was what I was here to do, today, if only she would notice the bloody capsule around Max's neck and remove the tiny piece of paper inside that contained my proposal.

Rachel snuggled into me, and I wrapped my arm around her, breathing in the delicious peachy smell of her hair.

"I can just see us sitting by our fire, with stockings hanging for all the children, mince pies for Santa, and me knitting in my rocking chair."

"You, knitting?" I laughed. The picture of Rachel knitting was too absurd.

"We would have to be married first though, wouldn't we?" I asked tentatively, my heart thumping in my chest.

"Well, yes, of course. Although I could start practising my knit one pearl one beforehand." She laughed, playing along with her own joke.

"What would you say?" I asked.

"What do you mean what would I say?"

"If I asked you to marry me?" My entire body fizzed as I said the words and I felt the goosebumps surface.

"You'd have to ask me to find out."

And then I froze.

I should have got down on one knee there and then, been brave and just asked her, but I couldn't. Fear took over, and the thought of her laughing at me, thinking that I was just larking about, made me freeze. There was an awkward silence and I just stared at the capsule on Max's collar, willing Rachel to notice it, to save me from this awkward moment, but she didn't. Instead, she suggested we head back.

"Shall we go and have a hot chocolate at your parents'?"

"Sure, I'm feeling a bit cold now to be honest," I replied, and so we headed back towards the car, meandering slowly along the path whilst we took in the view of dads and sons kicking footballs, children playing on the swings, and joggers running past.

We were chatting about the new art class I had recently joined as I reached into my pocket for the car keys. Rachel went to open the boot of my Ford Fiesta – the top sports model that Dad bought me for my twenty-first. It's a tight squeeze for Max, but he just lies down placidly in the boot for the ten-minute journey. Rachel had pulled out the fabric steps and was extending them from the lip of the boot for Max, when I approached to help her.

"What's Max got around his neck?" she asked, reaching for the pink sparkly pellet fixed to his collar.

"I don't know, open it and see." My heart was racing with anticipation again.

With her back to me, she carefully unscrewed the capsule and pulled out the tiny scrap of paper from inside.

She leant forwards and threw her arms around Max.

"Yes, of course I'll marry you, you fluffy doughnut." She laughed as I spun her around to face me.

"No, not him, me!"

Her face was perfect, her bright blue eyes as wide as saucers, with the expression of an excited schoolgirl.

"Yes."

The words travelled through me, bringing an overwhelming sense of comfort and safety. I had to force back the tears that were prickling the backs of my eyes, and I smiled as I held her.

"I love you, Rachel, more than you will ever know."

"I love you too."

We decided not to say anything to Mum and Dad. I told Rachel that I'd speak to her father, Derek, and ask him officially for permission. I might not have done things in the right order, but Rachel didn't seem perturbed by this. She understands that I get struck with anxiety sometimes, that I have more phobias than she has students in her class, but she doesn't judge me.

When I get one of my stress-induced migraines, Rachel always understands, pulling the curtains in my bedroom and settling me down with a cold compress and a glass of water before making my favourite meal of shepherd's pie, for when I'm feeling better. She even goes to the local shop to get me a bar of Galaxy since I always crave something sweet when I've had a migraine, feeling like I'm hung over for a good twenty-four hours afterwards.

With my recent promotion at work, there's been a notable increase in migraines. Rachel insists I should go to the doctor, but he'll only give me more medicine to shove in the back of my drawer, since they don't work. He'll probe with lots of questions that I won't give him answers to.

I know it's work, but I can't tell anyone – not even Rachel. I hate having more responsibility and I hate having to fake that I'm happy with the promotion. But Dad has arranged things, no doubt, to have me and Rachel kept close at hand so he can keep an eye on us, and massage his ego by setting our journey into coupledom on its way. I shouldn't complain – I wouldn't have been able to buy the engagement ring if it weren't for his financial help, the diamond which has now sealed our commitment to one another.

I still can't quite believe it… we're officially engaged to be married.

Chapter 3

RONNIE

I call up the stairs to Amanda who's soaking in the bath.

"I'll meet you at Rachel's later."

"Okay, don't be late, and wear a jacket."

James and Rachel have announced their engagement, and I feel slightly reluctant about meeting her parents this evening round at her place. I told Amanda that I've cancelled my snooker night, and that I need to pop by the office en route to Rachel's. I was never actually going to snooker; I was supposed to be seeing Penny since it's her birthday, so I need to go round and make my excuses. I'd rather do it in person than send her a text, I'm not a callous man. Plus, I have a gift I want to give her, and can't wait to see her reaction.

I enjoy pleasant surprises almost as much as practical jokes. Perhaps the two are intrinsically linked; that overriding feeling of glory as the recipient is astounded by a generous gift, like the moment of wonder when a magician reveals his best effect, rendering the audience speechless.

I keep my speed down as my hands grip the cold, soft leather steering wheel. The gritters have been out, but I'm not risking the other loonies on the road who don't know how to handle icy road conditions or have Pirelli tyres to compensate. Time is of the essence though, since it's going to take me a good twenty minutes to get over to Rachel's from Penny's.

Penny is thirty-five today, and I know she's expecting me to stay for dinner, but it's imperative that I put family first. She's aware of this and never makes a fuss.

Whilst I sometimes feel a twinge of guilt after our meetings, I'm a man, and have a man's needs. It's not my fault Amanda went off the boil when we hit our thirties. If I'm honest, she's never been particularly adventurous with sex, but it has become a chore nowadays, and only happens as often as she gets the oven cleaned, which is about once every six months. When she does capitulate, she usually lies there and thinks of England, doing her duty, but it's like making love to a wooden doll. I have tried romancing her; flowers arrive once a week (courtesy of Penny – she's a great secretary) and I make time regularly to take her out for dinner and spoil her a little. But, I guess it's to be expected, the sex just dries up in a marriage, especially when women approach the menopause. We have a great relationship in many other ways though, and I've never pleaded the *'My wife doesn't understand me'* defence since we have a good life and Amanda *does* understand me. We're both just set in our ways with a life that's comfortable and dependable, if not a little dull.

I've never pretended to Penny that I don't love Amanda, she knows I'm a family man and that she can never compete with that. We both take great lengths to be careful, of course. Nobody in the office knows about our affair, and I'm not the sort of guy who brags to his mates that I'm getting my leg over. Even my best mate Ray is totally unaware and I plan to keep it that way.

I pull into a parking space around the back of her block of apartments and wrap my mohair scarf around my neck, bracing for the cold as I leave my warmed seat. The chill signals that winter is setting in and my tennis weekends with Martyn are probably over.

Grabbing the flowers and gift bag from the boot of the car, I head towards the vestibule on the second floor where her apartment is. I say 'hers,' but it was a generous gift from me after her breakup with… what was his name? Rick or something. Well, after the breakup, she couldn't afford the rent where she was living and needed a fresh start. I managed to buy this place with some dividends I received two years ago, and she was over the moon. I'm not a fool though, it's in my name, but she stays here rent-free, which around this neck of the woods saves her the best part of a grand a month.

The doorbell echoes through the apartment. I have a key, but respect her privacy and have always wanted her to feel it's her home.

I know Penny sees other men, which is fine with me, and I trust her when she says she's far from ready to start another relationship. But, if I'm honest, I can't help feeling a twinge of jealousy when I know she's dating someone. She tries to hide all the signs, but I sense something different about her; she loses the edge on how much she wants to see me, and the *blow your mind sex* becomes *great sex*. She insists she can't imagine things any differently, that our arrangement suits her, but I guess she gets lonely sometimes. It's only fair that I let other men have a piece of her, since I'm having my cake and eating it – wife at home who manages all things domestic and always has my favourite plate waiting on the table, then a fuck buddy on the side who satisfies my carnal appetite.

I hear her high heels approaching the door and can sense her straightening her hair and checking her appearance is in place before opening it.

"Ronnie, you're early," she says. "I haven't even put the meat in the oven yet."

"That's fine, love, I need to explain," I say, already halfway through the door.

I kiss her on the lips, appreciating how she never wears lipstick when I'm coming round. I take in the roundness of her plump arse in a tight black and white gingham skirt, her pinched waist hidden under a tight black jumper. She looks classy, as always.

I place my gifts on the oval glass coffee table and take her in my arms.

"Something's come up, sweetheart. James and Rachel have announced their engagement and we're going over to Rachel's to meet her parents and celebrate."

I see the look of disappointment on her face. She pulls away from our embrace and heads towards the kitchen. She's trying to disguise the fact that she's upset, but I know she'll be fine once she opens my gift.

"No, don't make a coffee, Pen love, I have a bottle of something here. I can have a small glass with you." She turns and watches me as I pull the bottle of Bollinger from the bottle bag. I give her my best smile, trying to charm her to come back to me.

"I'll fetch two glasses then, sir." She winks at me, doing that thing she does, playing secretary and boss, which of course we are. She's forgiven me already.

The clock on the wall tells me that I don't have long; we won't have time for bedroom antics, not today. It would be unkind of me to even suggest it under the circumstances anyway.

Penny returns with two tall champagne flutes, eyeing the gifts that are on the table. As she pours our glasses with golden bubbles, I stop her before mine is half full, taking the glass and picking up the red and gold gift bag from the table. I raise my glass.

"Happy birthday, sweetheart."

Our glasses chime like a triangle sounding its moment of glory in an orchestral pause, and then I pass her the bag, trying my darndest to hide the smirk I can feel surfacing on my face. I've never gifted her something quite like this before.

Penny sits on the arm of my chair, teasing me as her skirt raises a little too high, exposing her silk stockings and enough thigh that it's hard for me to focus. She pulls the box out of the bag and gasps. It's a red and gold Cartier box which I hunted down on eBay and which, thankfully, arrived just in the nick of time.

Before she proceeds, I grab the box from her and slowly open it to reveal the diamond-encrusted panther bracelet. As she reaches for it, I snap the box shut. She jumps spectacularly. God! I've always wanted to re-enact that scene from *Pretty Woman*. Her giggle is contagious and we both chuckle as I hand the box over for her to take in the full beauty of the piece inside.

"Ronnie… this is too much!" she says.

"Sweetheart, you deserve it." I raise my glass again.

As she opens the clasp to place the bracelet around her delicate wrist, I wonder if she'll notice that it's second-hand. It's in excellent nick, and Emcy's did a great job of buffing it up and disguising any minor scratches. It's only a year or two old apparently, and clearly hasn't been worn much. If I know Penny, she'll probably get it valued before adding it to her home insurance. She won't care if it *is* second-hand when she discovers its worth.

The Panthère de Cartier collection ranges between £20,000 and £300,000. My face must have been a picture when I was told this one is worth £85,000. Yes, eighty-five smackeroonies. What's more, if she looks after it, it should increase in value too, although it could be a bit of a stumbling block that it doesn't have the original certificate.

"It's stunning," she says, twisting the white gold bracelet around her wrist with her slender fingers.

"It's white gold," I say, just in case she makes the mistake of believing it to be silver.

"I know," she says, her irritation obvious. "But, what are these stones?" She glides her long painted nails over the pavé diamonds set in the panther's head that's spotted with black stones.

"It's black onyx."

"Oh wow, and are these emeralds?" Her eyes widen in disbelief as she touches the bright green eyes, that almost match the shade of her own.

"They sure are," I say, delighted with her reaction to the birthday gift.

As she admires her new bracelet, I have a flashback to the bottle-blonde who sacrificed it at the poker game, and decide that Penny is far more worthy to be its owner. No doubt the woman had plenty more pieces of designer jewellery at home and probably had no idea of the value of this one.

I shuffle forward to sit on the edge of the cream leather armchair,

"Do you have to go already?" Penny asks, her disappointment clear.

"I'm so sorry, sweetheart, but I can't be late."

"But, I haven't thanked you properly for my present."
She kneels in front of me, stroking my knee. God, I wish
I had an extra half an hour to spare.

"You don't need to thank me, Penny, you deserve it,
my love. Besides, I promise we'll go out and celebrate
properly next week. You choose – anywhere you like."

Well, she knows I mean within reason. It must be
somewhere discreet; we usually dine in the city where we
can get lost in the crowd.

I reluctantly stand up, and Penny joins me. We fall
into an embrace, and she strokes my hair behind my ear,
just the way I like it. She stares into my eyes, questioning
one last time if I can stay a little longer. I touch her lips
with mine and she pulls me in for a deeper kiss. God, I
have never experienced a kiss like hers. The longing that
comes from her lips as her tongue expertly flicks around
my mouth drives me wild, even two years later. Her
passion is always as though it is our first kiss, reliving that
glorious moment in the lift after the work's Christmas
party when she grabbed my tie and pulled me in for a
full-on kiss, hungry and desperate. We had flirted a little
during the party, and I don't deny that I wanted it as
much as she did, but the way she took control and took
that risky first step excited me beyond belief. We ended
up jumping into a cab together, going back to hers, and
the rest is history, as they say.

"Now, be a good girl," I say, chuckling as I pull away.
I can't afford to let desire win on this occasion, I'm going
to be late as it is. "I love you, sweetheart."

"I love you too, Ronnie."

There are different kinds of love, I believe. I *do* mean it when I say I love her. It's a love with restraint though – on both our parts. We choose not to fall into that whole complacency thing, the point where the bubble bursts and the sexual tension begins to fade. Let's face it, most relationships go down that path eventually. But we manage to keep it alive. It's clearly helped by the fact that we only grab time to meet each other once or twice a month, and absence certainly does make the heart grow fonder. We choose to let our heads rule our hearts, lust over our conscience, but most of all we maintain a great friendship.

Penny has a certain sophistication that Amanda lacks. She's the kind of woman who never leaves the house without her makeup on, eyebrows perfectly groomed and high heels on – even indoors. She keeps herself in great shape, has curves in all the right places and, above all, is terrific fun, both at the dinner table *and* in the bedroom. She's simple, not complicated like so many women.

I'm not the easiest of people to get along with, I know, but she gets me. She puts up with my childish streak, like when I stuffed the pillows under the duvet the last time I stayed – I placed them full length under the duvet, with a grey fur cushion from her lounge peeping out the top to look like a tuft of hair.

Once hidden inside her wardrobe, I woke her by knocking on the door, and with the dim light from the hallway, could just make her out through the slats. She rolled over to hug me and snuggle in, before throwing the duvet back and shouting,

"You bastard, Ronnie! Why didn't you tell me you were leaving?"

I then waited for her to get comfortable again, listening to her mutter a few expletives, before springing out of the wardrobe, butt naked. It was brilliant – her scream was loud enough to wake the entire block, which was shortly followed by our rolling around with laughter. Yes, Penny is always a good sport.

People would presume that she's with me for my money. Yes, of course she gets treated very well, we fine dine, and she gets occasional lavish gifts, but after two years, I believe she has grown to love me in her own way. She tells me it's sexy that I'm ten years older, and that she loves my blunt and no-nonsense attitude she witnesses in the office. Best of all, she has *never* so much as hinted that she wants more from me. She has never suggested that I should leave Amanda.

After our fond goodbyes at the door, I tear myself away and put my trench coat on as I hurry towards the car. Guilty conscience suddenly kicks in, and I glance around the dimly-lit car park, tilting my head up to the specks of light coming from the windows in the apartment block. Nobody's looking, but I always have a sense that perhaps someone, somewhere, is watching.

The lights flash as I press the button to disarm the car alarm, and I slide into the cold leather driver's seat. I flick on the heated seats and turn the key. The dash lights up, welcoming me back, and the engine purrs like a contented cat.

I suppose you could say this baby is my other mistress. There's something strangely comforting, but also extremely sexy about the mix of undisputed luxury with the hidden power of a V12 engine under the bonnet. There's a reason why Bond had eight Aston Martin models during film making. It's indisputably the most classic car of all time, and I like the fact he never had one in storm black; I'm a black or white kind of man in life, as well as with my choice of car. Its glossy black shell highlights the curves and lines of the car better than any other colour.

Yes, this beauty may be worth three of Penny's new panther bracelet, but it's my most treasured pleasure and one that I have absolutely no guilt about.

Chapter 4

JAMES

After picking Mum up en route, I greet my beautiful fiancée with a deep kiss and tell her how great she looks.

"Enough of the sweet talk," Rachel says, "can you set the table while I get the garlic bread sorted?"

"You know Dad hates garlic bread," I say, heading towards the kitchen.

"Well, he doesn't have to eat it then, does he?"

I love how she's never intimidated by my father. Most people have this unspoken adoration for him, a little frightened by his success and his aura of confidence, but to Rachel, he's just your average man, and she never rises to his taunts or tantrums. Mum is used to him too; she just pacifies him like a mother would a child and has learnt how to expertly navigate his anger when it arises, with smooth and deft precision.

"Is there anything I can do to help?" Mum comes into the kitchen looking like a spare part, waiting for the arrival of Rachel's parents.

"No, we have it all under control. Grab yourself a glass and get some wine down you," Rachel says. "Mum and Dad will be here any minute, they're so looking forward to meeting you."

"Okay, if you're sure." Mum strokes Bella, Rachel's cat.

"Come on, beautiful. You come with me." Mum lifts the white cat, which jumps from her arms and heads over towards me.

"It's food time," I say, "bloody fickle furball."

I'm not really a cat person, and the loss of our family dog Max recently broke both my and Mum's hearts. He was a part of our family for as long as I can remember, and I'll never forget the day when Mum first brought him home.

I was only ten at the time, and not having any brothers or sisters, Max became more than just a family pet. He was like my best buddy, my soulmate. I would let him lie on my bed at night, loving the warmth of his heavy paw resting on my arm and feeling his twitches as he dreamt. I would talk to him, and imagine he absorbed every word that I said. His beautiful amber eyes would stare deep into my soul, like he knew me, he understood me – better than anyone else. Best of all, he made me feel safe. I would drop off to sleep secure in the knowledge that should anyone, or anything, intrude on my space, he would be the first to let me know.

The doorbell buzzes annoyingly. I hate how Rachel's apartment doesn't have a doorbell that chimes like normal doorbells do. I can't wait until we get a place together and we don't have to constantly relocate from

41

hers to mine. A few of my bits are scattered around her bathroom and bedroom but if it wasn't for the damn cat, I suspect she would have moved into my flat by now, which is far more comfortable than her pad. But, she insists that we wait until we get a small house together since she wants a garden for Bella — which seems ridiculous as this flat only has a postage stamp balcony where the cat occasionally lies to grab some sporadic moments of sun.

Rachel is a tad old-fashioned, which I find so endearing. I know she feels her parents would be more comfortable with us living together once we're married, but I hope being engaged will suffice.

"I've got it," I say, dashing towards the front door, smiling at Mum who looks particularly nervous. She hovers by the worn beige sofa that Rachel insists is grey.

"James, darling." Carole's cold cheek meets mine as she kisses me 'European-style'. Her fur coat feels as though she's been on some arctic mission, and I usher her in to get out of the cold stairwell.

"I suppose I should call you son, now." Derek greets me with a handshake, as if formally inviting me to become his future son-in-law. I help him remove his coat and scarf and hang both his and Carole's coats in the single cloaks cupboard.

"Come in, Mum's itching to meet you," I say. "Dad's been delayed at the office but will be here soon."

I glance nervously at my watch, annoyed to see that he's late. It would have been nice if he had been on time for once. He should be here to welcome them with Mum who's clearly out of her comfort zone tonight. I so want it all to go well; if Rachel's parents don't like Mum and Dad, it may taint their opinion of me, and their acceptance of me as part of their family.

It's my worst nightmare introducing people to my dad. He can be such a clown, and whilst he thinks it funny to make jibes about people, always vying to be centre of attention, he comes across as arrogant sometimes. He promised me that he won't fool about tonight, and that he'll refrain from his usual table antics. I don't think shoving the cream in Derek's nose asking him if it smells 'off' would go down too well.

"Mum, this is Carole and Derek," I say nervously.

Stupid! Of course, they know each other's names. Both sides have had the full rundown on career, background, family relations, likes and dislikes. It was like the Spanish Inquisition when Mum and Dad interrogated me about Rachel's family from the moment they realised we were getting serious.

Being an only child comes with pressures, and being a son even more so. It's like I'm the bloody heir to the throne the way Dad always bangs on about me having the business one day. My knowing that it's not what I want, has always left me feeling like I'm not good enough. This is exacerbated by the pressure of knowing my future choice of wife has to be good enough too, and, if I'm honest, had Rachel not met their approval, I would

43

have gone ahead with it anyway; I know she's the one for me.

"Hello, I've heard so much about you, Rachel is always singing your praises," Mum says, greeting Carole with an awkward kiss. They smile as they eye each other up and down, in the way that women do.

"Amanda, so lovely to meet you at last." Derek stoops to greet her with a kiss, turning on a charming smile I've never seen before. "We can't wait to have your son as part of our family, I've taken quite a shine to him, you know."

I'm a bit baffled by this statement. There's always a sense of being analysed by Derek; he seems to turn me inside out with the way he looks at me, as if he were a professional psychologist. The sense of unease I feel when around him could be my paranoia, but nonetheless I've always sensed he's not quite sure about me. He asks so many questions, and I'm not a wear-your-heart-on-your-sleeve type of guy.

When I plucked up the courage to ask him for his daughter's hand in marriage I stammered and stuttered like an idiot. The way he looked at me, I thought for a moment he was going to say no. It was like the moment before one of Dad's pranks is revealed. My hands were clammy, my heart was trying to burst out of my chest until he finally smiled and said, "Yes, of course. I know you'll look after my little girl."

This was followed up by a *'get to know your son-in-law'* session, where Derek quizzed me with endless questions.

I know he only wants to get to know me, but it takes a lot for me to open up, and I like to keep my safety barrier in place. I think of it like the world's invisible forcefield that supposedly protects us from 'killer electrons'. Dad has always said that 'knowledge is power', so I believe that the more information you give to someone, the greater power it gives them, with shit-loads of electrons to weaken your defences.

It takes a long time for me to get to know a person, and even longer to develop trust, which is why Rachel is my perfect woman. She never pushes. I'm allowed to just be me, and if I don't feel like talking, she doesn't probe. She allows me to unravel in my own time and is content to take the rest of our lives to get to know each other and each other's secrets.

Everyone makes themselves comfortable on the two sofas either side of the coffee table. Mum, Rachel and I sit together facing Carole and Derek, as if they are a couple about to be interviewed for a job. My right hand makes its way to my mouth automatically and I nibble on my fingernail which is already worn down to the quick.

"So, Rachel told us about your wonderful home, and the stables," Carole says.

Rachel nudges me in the ribs, my cue to sort out drinks for everyone.

"We'll save the champagne until Dad gets here, but can I get you both something to drink?" I say, cringing at how nervous I sound, and interrupting Mum who was mid-flow with her response to Carole.

"Just a soft drink for me, and a glass of red for Derek, if you have it?" Carole says.

Derek stops her. "No, I'll wait until your father arrives," he says, looking at his wristwatch.

"I'm so sorry, I'll send him a text and check he's on his way," Mum says by way of an apology, and we give each other a look which confirms that we're *both* feeling the frustration that Dad isn't here. His absence is like an elephant in the room – a larger than life grey elephant with red spots who may as well be wearing swimming trunks. Typical of Dad to want to make a grand entrance.

I loosen my collar, feeling clammy with nerves. The smell of food filling the kitchen space is making me feel queasy. My heart feels like it's about to burst through my chest, and I take a few deep breaths.

I'm not usually like this with Rachel's parents, but having them meet my parents feels so intimate; they'll probably learn more about me this evening than they have in the past year that I've known them. If Dad decides to embarrass me with tales of my childhood this evening, I'll be mortified. Rachel understands I went through a rebellious phase in my teens; she knows about the drugs I took at college and throwing up over the interior of Dad's new Jaguar when he picked me up from my first party aged sixteen. But Dad loves to relish those occasions; he took great pleasure in telling Rachel how I wet myself at school once, when the fire alarm sounded right above my head.

I take some breathing space in the kitchen, where I pour a glass of orange juice for Carole, and grab myself a bottle of beer.

Once back in the lounge area, I smile at Mum. She looks so lovely tonight. Her outfit makes her look feminine and glamourous and I think how much it suits her. It's mainly the fact that she's wearing a dress, but her hair looks different too; she's wearing it down for a change, and it makes her look younger, as does the unfamiliar makeup.

I always remember her picking me up from school in jodhpurs and riding boots and I used to hate how she stood out from the other mothers. They were always dressed up to the nines with their Versace jeans and Christian Dior saddle bags, with perfect hair and manicured nails, whilst Mum always rocked up in her scruffy, worn gilet, and mud-encrusted muck boots, with strands of hay poking out of her jumper. But that's Mum, confident with who she is, and happy with the simple things in life – like animals and nature.

I wish I could be more like her, finding the confidence to accept who I am, and how I look. There's always a sense of lack with me, especially when I'm around Dad, which I find so hard to put into words. He tells me he's proud of me, but deep down I just don't believe him. Why would I? I'm a fraud. He thinks I love working for the firm, and believes I'm happy with the promotion he arranged for me. But the reality is, I don't like having more responsibility, I'm not like him, and I hate bossing people about.

I only joined the company because I felt under pressure. Mum said I needed to find a job after I flunked my grades at college and said that I should start paying my way. I dossed around for six months before Dad somehow manipulated things so that if I were to join his business, he would help me with my first flat. It was a no-brainer; I had to gain some experience and start somewhere, and I was desperate to have my own place. Besides, I had to make it up to him somehow for failing to go to uni.

If I'm honest, I still don't really know what I want to do in life and if I did, I would have no idea how to take the helm and steer towards it. I always loved art and graphics at school, but Dad insisted that if I was to go to uni then I should take a business degree and said I was wasted with *'arty farty'* stuff. As much as I wanted to please him, make him proud of me, I couldn't face three years doing something *he* wanted me to do, so that is why it became my mission to avoid uni at all costs. I will never *be* like him, and I don't know when he'll realise that.

I pass the glass of orange juice to Carole, and Rachel beckons me over with her warm smile, inviting me to sit down next to her. She puts her hand on my knee and I take in the strange sight of seeing the ring on her hand. I still can't believe she said 'yes'. The ring on her finger makes me feel complete somehow. It gives me some assurance that I'm headed in the right direction, and that is all that matters for now. A life with somebody that I love, and who loves me back as an equal.

Chapter 5

RONNIE

"Hi, come in. My parents are already here."

Rachel greets me at the door, dressed in a green silk dress with black lace trim and a simple gold necklace set in the V of its neckline. Her thick auburn hair has had a few inches chopped since I last saw her, and hangs in a sharp-edged bob. Her smooth fresh face radiates warmth, with her makeup failing to obscure her adorable freckle-peppered nose.

"So sorry if I'm late, I got delayed at the office a bit longer than expected." I hand her the mixed bouquet that I made a quick pit stop for at the garage up the road.

"No, no, you're fine," she says. "Let me take your coat."

As she helps me remove my trench coat I notice the smell of the litter tray in the bathroom. Who the heck has a cat in a high level flat? In fact, who has a cat? Bloody fickle creatures, always rubbing up against you when they want something. Unpredictable too. Last time I was here and stroked Bella, she was purring and fussing one minute, then dug her claws into me the next; don't trust the damn predators.

"James, your dad is here," Rachel says. James pops his head out from the lounge doorway.

"Hiya, Pops, we're in here."

Well, I don't know where else they would be!

Rachel's cramped apartment is modest to say the least. An open plan lounge-kitchen-cum-diner, with a tiny bathroom – minus the bath. A boxy double bedroom and that's it. I hope now they're engaged they'll move in together, and if James sells his flat, they should be able to get a small house together. I'll help them, of course, by way of a healthy deposit – an engagement present – but will save that news for another time, I wouldn't want to make Rachel or her parents feel awkward. James has warned me to behave myself tonight.

Rachel's parents are standing in the lounge, waiting to greet me.

"Hi, Ronnie. So lovely to meet you at last," Carole says, in a surprisingly plummy accent. "I've heard so much about you."

"All bad, I hope." I laugh as I greet her with a peck on the cheek while I take in her husband who is waiting with his hand poised.

His handshake is firm. I like that. It says a lot about a person; I can't be doing with one of those soft limp shakes that feels like a lettuce tickling your palm.

"Great to meet you, Derek," I say, reassured that he is nothing like I had pictured him.

51

"And you," Derek says in a deep voice, not giving away any social standing with his accent just yet.

He is shorter than me, which I like. Probably in his fifties, which I like even more. I can see where his daughter gets her kind eyes from, and he has an understated sophistication about him with his smart checked shirt collar showing under his unbranded black wool sweater. He's wearing chinos and Derby shoes, and I recognise the hint of bergamot that tells me he wears the same Calvin Klein aftershave as James. He's wearing a blazer, which triggers my memory. Damn! I forgot my jacket. I just hope my smart chinos and Ralph Lauren sweater will appease Amanda.

"Amanda was just telling us about losing your beloved Max last week, it's awful when we lose our pets," he says, now revealing he equals his wife with his 'ever so slightly plummy' accent.

Amanda has taken the loss of Max, our German Shepherd, really badly, and despite still having our chocolate Lab, Daisy, I know it won't be long before she'll want a replacement for Max. I glance in her direction and she smiles at me in a way that tells me she's annoyed. Damn! I don't know why, since she isn't usually one for dressing up.

"Sweetheart, I'm sorry I'm a bit late," I say, approaching to give her the customary peck on her cheek.

She's released her hair from its horsey plait for a change, leaving her bleached hair to cascade loosely over her shoulders. I'm surprised to see her wearing a dress, although she *is* wearing long black leather riding boots which gives it a tomboyish feel.

Rachel interrupts us all with a bottle of bubbly and the flowers beautifully arranged in a large glass vase that she places on the centre of the coffee table.

"Dad, a glass of Moët?" James says, pouring me a glass.

"Only a little, son, I've got to drive."

"You'll be alright to have one or two?" he says, questioning my reluctance. "Besides, you can always get a taxi with Mum, then she can drive you over to pick up your car tomorrow."

I nod in agreement, knowing full well there is no way I will be leaving my pride and joy in the car park overnight, not in this neck of the woods. Rachel's flat is in a built-up area in Staines, not the most desirable of places, and I secretly hope that with the engagement it won't be too long before she and James will be moving closer towards us, somewhere a little more upmarket.

"Show us the ring then," I say, pretending that I've never seen it before. James showed it to me before the big proposal. I suggested he replaced the ring in the box with a plastic ring, like one of those you get in a Christmas cracker, but he wasn't impressed. I said he could have quickly given her the real one straight after, but he wasn't onboard with the idea. I couldn't help but feel it was a missed opportunity for a great *What the fuck?* moment.

"It's not the time to be playing practical jokes, Dad," James had said.

Rachel presents her hand proudly to me, dimples marking her cheeks as she gives an excited giggle.

"Not bad for Poundland," I say, taking in the triple diamond set ring, embedded in white gold to make the diamonds look larger than they are. I know it set James back just over a grand; he asked me for an advance from next month's pay and I insisted on knowing what it was for.

"Well, they say diamonds are a girl's best friend," I say, as I return her infectious smile. "I'm so pleased for you both."

"Shall we raise our glasses to James and Rachel?" I get up from my seat to raise my glass and everyone follows my lead, standing to salute the newly engaged couple.

"Here's to James and Rachel."

"Yes, here's to *Rachel* and James," Derek says pointedly.

"Have you set a date yet?" Carole asks, looking lovingly at her daughter.

James is a lucky man. He's done well for himself. Rachel is a very balanced girl; well-educated with a sensible head on her shoulders. She's a little older than James, but with brains *and* beauty, I know they'll make a great couple. She's got a cheeky side to her too, and we get on great. I already think of her as a daughter and she won me over the moment I realised she is onside when I play my jokes.

"They've only just announced the engagement," Amanda says.

"Oh really? I thought you mentioned something about next spring?" Carole says, almost gloating because she clearly has more information than we do.

Rachel and James look awkward.

"Well, we thought we might like a May wedding. I know it's only seven months away, but with Rachel in charge, we won't be hanging around," James says, with some uncertainty. He seems nervous, reluctant to sit down as if he doesn't know which side to sit on. He hovers by the coffee table while the rest of us sit comfortably on the sofas.

"May doesn't give your dad much chance to save up," I say playfully, looking at Derek.

"Ronnie." Amanda jabs me in the side with her elbow. "Of course, we insist that we contribute in some way, but I'm sure we can discuss that another time."

"Yes, of course," I add obediently, feeling like a chastised schoolboy. Well, honestly. I don't get it. In the old days, the father of the bride always paid for the wedding. I'm not tight, and of course, I *will* contribute, but I do hate it when customs die out. Take Sundays for example, it's supposed to be a family day – a day for switching off from the world and relaxing with a good book and a roast dinner. These days everyone dashes about shopping, working, and it blends into being like every other day of the week.

"We have a savings account that's been building over the years for Rachel's big day," Derek says with pride.

Of course they have.

It's where Rachel gets her organisational skills from. A trait of being an accountant's daughter. I bet they have their Christmas fund, funerals and legal fees for any unforeseen emergency possible, neatly stashed away. No, there won't be any catastrophe or occasion unaccounted for in their house. But better that way, I suppose, than living hand to mouth; he obviously earns a decent wage, and Carole is a teacher, apparently. Meticulous saving is obviously not their only strength either; they've done a cracking job with Rachel and I know she will be good for James. He has probably been a little spoilt over the years and can get a little carried away with credit cards. I've bailed him out once or twice, but since he's been with Rachel things seem to have calmed down, thankfully.

I didn't have time for a cigarette before arriving, and am about to head out of the patio doors to the tiny balcony when Rachel says, "Shall we sit down for dinner?"

I'd almost forgotten we were having dinner, but the gnawing discomfort in the pit of my stomach reminds me I haven't eaten since lunchtime.

We all cram around the undersized Ikea table. James brings in two chairs from the balcony to make up for the lack of seating, and we engage in general small talk whilst Rachel and James pair up to bring the food to the table. They make a great team.

"Well, this looks fabulous," I say convincingly.

It's lasagne. I'm more your meat and two veg kind of man and can't stand anything remotely fancy. Amanda knows me well, and always gives me what I like – steak and chips, or bangers and mash.

"Ronnie…" Carole offers me the garlic bread and I politely decline. I hate garlic, or anything that's spoilt with too many spices.

Amanda gives me the stare, which is unnecessary. I'm not short-sighted enough to say something inappropriate in front of the outlaws. I've already complimented their daughter on the huge dish of bubbling lasagne topped with browned cheese, and I have no intention of removing the stopper on the salt dispenser to surprise someone with a little extra seasoning.

I listen to the tedious conversation as Amanda and Carole get to know each other. Just my luck that Carole likes horses too! They ramble on about how many 'hands' their horses measure, and I learn that Carole doesn't have her own paddock and stables like Amanda. She explains how she hires a horse from her best friend's yard, and mucks it out twice a week, riding it at weekends. It seems more of a hobby, unlike Amanda who has the luxury of making it her full-time (unpaid) job, spending all her days out in the field with the dogs and her horses. Well, *dog* – now that Max has gone. She has a couple of stablehands, Belinda and Stacey, and with two horses of her own, and another one that she is currently trying out, she may as well open a riding school.

Sometimes, I think her sweat smells of those damn horses. But it keeps her happy; she does her thing and I do mine.

I am soon bored with the evening and having told Derek all about Back Up and how we recently rejected an offer from a large well-known security company to buy out the firm, I start to think about Penny, imagining us at Antonio's, her favourite little Italian, next week. I'm ninety-nine percent sure it's the restaurant she'll choose. I picture her in a slinky little number, showing me just enough of her luscious cleavage to tease me and I have to stop myself before I get a semi under the table. She may be like sex on a stick, but it's more than that. I've never been a one-night stand kind of guy; you may as well hire a prostitute if it's a question of just needing a quick shag. No, I like the whole wining and dining experience, and I like to feel needed, wanted. The riskiness of our rendezvous is a mix of nerves and excitement, but I know it's dangerous. I would never want my family to discover that I'm cheating on Amanda.

I'm itching for a cigarette, and ask if I can be excused from the table now that we've finished the delicious lemon meringue pie that Rachel made.

"Of course, Ronnie, I'll get you something to use as an ashtray," Rachel says, ever the perfect hostess.

I receive the customary look of disapproval from Amanda as well as a pitying look from Derek as Carole takes his dessert dish to help clear the table.

"You should give that up, it'll kill you," Derek says, one eyebrow raised. Sanctimonious git! Tell me something I don't know.

"Well, we're all dying anyway," I say, tucking my chair under the table. "We all have our vices, don't we?"

"I suppose so," Derek says, to pacify me. Somehow, I can't imagine him having many vices. Not as many as me, at any rate.

Addiction is so annoying. You find something you enjoy, and before you know it, it has a hold of you. The more you do it, the less effect it has, so you slide down the slippery slope of doing it more and more. Take my practical jokes, for example. It started with everyday little pranks, such as pretending the cream is off and placing my spoon under James's nose to get him to do the sniff test, before shoving the cream on the tip of his nose, or sticking a plastic spider on the toilet roll for unsuspecting guests, and then there was the time I bought a second remote control without Amanda knowing. I had her going for nearly a week, confused how the volume kept changing or the channel mysteriously switched over. But these jokes seem too childish and obvious now. I don't get the same buzz as I did in the early days, plus everyone that knows me gets tired of the same old jokes. No, I find myself suddenly wanting a bigger kick. Like the first nicotine hit you get in the morning which makes your blood pressure soar and heart rate increase.

It's not long before the devil on my shoulder strikes again. Whilst I'm puffing on my cigarette out on the cold, dimly-lit balcony, Rachel comes out to join me, in a thick fleece jacket to keep her warm. Bella is snuggled in her arms. She sits down to join me.

"Aren't you cold, Ronnie? Do you want me to get your coat?"

"No, sweetheart, you've done enough waiting on me tonight, I'll fetch it," I say, resting my cigarette on the edge of the green ceramic saucer that is my makeshift ashtray.

The balcony is only about six feet square, with a metal railing that overlooks a drop of about seventy feet. Just as I make to leave, James comes out to join us, and Bella jumps down from Rachel's lap. I rush to pick her up. Stroking her behind the ears, I realise she has literally just jumped into my next great machination.

"Aw, I think perhaps Bella is taking a liking to me after all."

Rachel smiles at me and Bella.

Back in the lounge everyone is relaxing on the sofa drinking cups of coffee, and as I walk through the room to go and fetch my coat, Amanda stops me. "Haven't you finished that cigarette yet?" she says.

"Don't nag, dear, I'm just fetching my coat." I give a small sigh.

In the entrance hall, I put the cat down and quickly pull my coat on, grabbing Bella before she makes her escape. Then I place her in the tiny cloakroom cupboard where my coat had been a few seconds earlier, and close the door. I don't want her spoiling my plan.

60

Back in the lounge, everyone is engrossed in deep conversation about what seems set to be the 'wedding of the year'. I slide discreetly into the kitchen without being noticed, and quickly grab the extra-large white tea towel from the towel hooks. I arrange it in a heap in the crook of my arm, tucking it in, and then I hold my other arm across, petting it with gentle tenderness.

Returning to the patio, I'm glad to discover that James and Rachel are still chatting; it seems they are already making plans to start looking for a new home and James has had a valuation on his flat.

After picking up the remains of my cigarette, I move towards the railings, angling myself a little so that I give nothing away. Rachel glances in my direction and smiles at me, believing I'm still stroking her precious Bella, before continuing her conversation with my son. Then, I put on the performance of the year.

I start coughing and sputtering as if choking on something, and once I have the attention of both of them, I lean against the railings.

"Ronnie, are you okay?" Just as Rachel rises from her seat to attend to me, I give a spectacular final cough, choking up my pretend furball at the same time as dropping the tea towel from my arms over the balcony. Rachel switches from concerned daughter-in-law to horrified mother. She clutches at the railings and we both stare down towards the distant pavement below, lit dimly enough that the white splat on the pavement easily plays its role of a squashed cat. Ending my coughing fit, I show my shock.

"Rachel, I'm so…" But she's fled, screaming through the lounge towards the door. James follows her and the conversation stops dead. Everyone's faces are frozen in confusion as I head past them to chase after James and Rachel. They're too quick for me; the lift has already gone and I imagine their panic as they descend to the ground floor.

I quickly re-enter the flat and grab the cat from the cupboard to be greeted by Amanda. "What's going on?" she asks, clearly concerned.

"Nothing, just a little joke," I say, going back to the lift which has now arrived. I enter the empty lift and place the cat down before pressing the ground floor button and quickly jumping out again, leaving the cat to descend to greet its owners for their journey back up,

"Ronnie, what the hell have you done?" Amanda says. I push past her to return to the balcony, reassuring Carole and Derek that everything's fine.

I peer over the railings to discover the white tea towel has vanished. They must be on their way back already.

Back in the vestibule, I hear the mechanics of the lift in motion and I wait for the double doors to open. This could all go horribly wrong if someone else in the block calls the lift and the cat dashes out on the wrong floor. But there's always risk, with any good practical joke. It's what makes the adrenalin pump even faster. I hold my breath, praying that Rachel and James will have the cat with them, my heart beating fast and my legs trembling. I hear the familiar chime as the lift reaches our floor, and brace myself for their reaction.

The cat is cradled in Rachel's arms. Her glassy-eyed stare tells me she is not happy with me.

"You bastard, Ronnie," she says, striding past me towards the flat, where Amanda is waiting at the door.

"Nice one, Dad," James says, with a hint of sarcasm in his voice.

Amanda shakes her head at me as I enter the flat.

"Did you have to make such a scene tonight? We've only just met them." The words are barely audible as she mutters them through clenched teeth under her breath.

"Oh, chill," I say, "you know I can't resist the opportunity for a little practical joke."

Back in the lounge, the atmosphere is a tad awkward. Carole and Derek are looking bewildered, as Rachel sits on the corner of the settee holding the cat tightly and rubbing her face against its fur. Thankfully, James comes to my rescue.

"My dad's always been a bit of a practical joker. Honestly, he drives us all crazy."

That's my boy, always gets my jokes, although I sense even *he* is a little disturbed by my latest triumph. Carole and Derek look at each other.

"I'm sorry, Rachel," I say insincerely, as I sit next to her and put my arm around her shoulders, trying not to laugh. "I would never harm an animal, especially your Bella. Will you forgive me?" I'm trying my hardest not to burst into a fit of the giggles. It's a combination of just how well the joke went, as well as my compulsion to laugh in awkward situations. It could be nerves or something, but I often laugh at the most inappropriate times as if the little devil inside has Tourette's.

Rachel gives me a half smile. James is taking delight in explaining to Carole and Derek some of my tamer practical jokes and Amanda is pouring herself another glass of bubbles. No doubt I'm in for a bollocking later.

"I'll get you back one day," Rachel says. "You just wait and see how it is when the shoe is on the other foot." The smile edging its way to the corners of her mouth tells me that I'm forgiven.

Chapter 6

JAMES

Rachel and I have decided to hold off on the wedding. We've been up to our eyes in boxes and preparing our new home over the last few months. We found a three-bedroomed terraced house in Leatherhead, which is a bit cheaper than most areas around here but gives us one more bedroom than we had hoped for. It's nothing grand, but friends of our age are finding it hard to get on the property ladder, so I should be grateful.

Dad gave us a large input of cash for a deposit – probably his 'guilt' money after the stupid prank he pulled on our engagement night in front of Rachel's parents. But that's what he does, causes chaos and then finds a way to compensate if he happens to hurt or upset anyone in the process. I'm convinced that Rachel underplayed her upset to help placate any concerns her parents had. She ended up laughing with Dad and scheming ways that she would get him back one day. I thank God that Carole and Derek haven't mentioned it again since.

Dad was always the fun one when I was a child. He spent hours playing games with me – although there was always something to risk. Either a forfeit or some other sacrifice was given to the loser, he could never play just for fun.

When I think about it, it was an ingenious way to get me to carry out household chores. If I lost at rummy, I would have to set the table for dinner all week or unload the dishwasher; that was preferable to having to stand up in a restaurant and recite some poem or song that Dad set me as a forfeit.

We played some great jokes on Mum in my youth too, which I readily admit I enjoyed. I particularly loved the egg prank: we would place a hard-boiled egg back in the egg carton and watch with anticipation as she cracked the eggs to make an omelette. We would laugh until the tears streamed down our faces, and Mum would just raise her eyebrows with a quiet grin on her face, shaking her head as if we were both two naughty schoolboys.

I remember the brilliant games of hide and seek we played too. I used to get the better of Dad – being I was much smaller than him and could squeeze into the tiniest of spaces. He had to give up looking one time when I hid in the cupboard under the kitchen sink. I was only nine, and had planned ahead: I'd removed the cleaning items from their place and hidden them behind the dried foods in another cupboard. I won't pretend it was easy, thirty minutes crouched in a 'squashed cat' yoga-like pose killed my back, and my neck ached for days afterwards. But, when I finally came out to find Dad sitting in the TV room watching the tennis, saying he'd given up, I felt magnificent for a moment. I had beaten him; something I'd never succeeded at before.

"Well done, you got me,'" he said, keeping his eyes glued to the TV.

I remember the feeling of anticlimax as it dawned on me how he didn't celebrate my victory in quite the same way we did with his. No matter whether it was a game of Monopoly, or one of his spur-of-the-moment pranks, he always smiled like the Cheshire cat praising himself for such an original stunt and insisting that I learn to take it in my stride; 'Be a good sport,' he would always say when he saw my sulky face, or threatening tears.

The time I remember the most was when Robert came over to play. I think this was the turning point for me since I felt too grown up for Dad's childish pranks and didn't want to play along anymore.

Robert and I were best friends and met in junior school. I loved hanging out with him; he always seemed to be into the same stuff as me, without being annoying. We swapped Pokémon cards, and raced our remote-control cars up and down the road where he lived, often having sleepovers at each other's houses. I think we were around twelve at the time and were growing out of making camps and kicking a football around, more interested in PlayStation games, or nicking one of Dad's cigarettes and smoking it down at the stables. But on this day, we were bored and ambitiously checking whether the pool in our garden seemed warm enough for a swim.

The sun was shimmering off the water, and it looked so inviting, but it was cold. The cover had only been removed the day before and the heating had been switched on, but Mum said it would take around forty-eight hours until it would be warm enough to swim. The pump was humming in the wooden power shed, and streams of water bubbled through the filters as it circulated the chemicals Dad had put in earlier.

Robert removed his socks and sat on the tiled edge to dip his toes in.

"It's freezing," he said, retracting his toes. His shoulders slouched as he returned to sit on the sun lounger and watch me.

I was standing on the edge of the diving board, picturing myself in a few days' time, springing off the board into a racing dive to swim a full length of the pool underwater. I imagined the water wrapped around me, the silence as I held my breath to reach the far wall, the taste of chlorine on my lips.

The patio doors on the terrace opened, and Dad came out, holding his rifle. We often used to shoot down tin cans together with round-nosed pellets, but it struck me as odd that he had no target with him.

"I dare you to jump in," he said, calling from about twenty-five metres away from where I stood.

"Er, no, I've got my clothes on," I said, looking at Robert and raising my eyebrows the way Mum always did.

Robert shielded his forehead from the sun with his hand, and his eyes shifted towards Dad with the look of a frightened deer. I turned around to be greeted by the sight of Dad pointing the rifle directly at me as he slowly approached.

"Ten seconds, or I'll shoot," he said, teasing me. He would often tease or threaten me… only the week before, he had pretended to get an electric shock from a loose wire on a lamp in the gym. He had given an Oscar-winning performance, writhing around on the floor having a fit before I noticed the damn thing wasn't even plugged in.

"No," I said, "besides, you'd miss anyway." I wanted to appear confident in front of Robert, and I knew Dad was bluffing.

He started counting backwards from ten, and I reassured Robert who seemed fixated on watching Dad.

"He's only bluffing," I said, balancing my feet on the edge of the board, leaning carefully so that I didn't fall in. As I turned to face Dad, his countdown ended.

"Three, two, one!"

The sting was such an unexpected shock. I fell dramatically into the pool. The impact of the icy water took my breath away, and I surfaced, coughing and spluttering. I started screaming, swallowing mouthfuls of water as I swam towards the steps. Robert rushed to give me a hand, helping me up the ladder, then holding me as I limped to the sun lounger, where I sat down and began crying hysterically.

"He shot me." The words were fragmented between sobs, and Robert edged my hand away from where it was pressed on my thigh. There was blood seeping through my jeans like dark burgundy ink. The shock that Dad had shot me intensified, crazing my mind like a swarm of bees attacking me, whilst my leg felt numb in comparison.

"It's not bleeding much," Robert said, fear written all over his face.

Dad entered the pool area just as Mum arrived on the scene. My hysterics increased.

"Dad shot me!" I wailed like a baby, panicking that someone needed to call an ambulance.

"It was only Blu Tack," Dad replied, laughing. "It won't have done any harm."

Blu Tack?

I felt a complete idiot. My reaction had been as though a bullet had just entered my leg, the main artery damaged, with impending need of an urgent amputation. But as I calmed down, I realised it was just a mild sting, and the bees cleared from my head.

I stood up and pulled my jeans down to see a graze with droplets of blood seeping from it.

"It's just a flesh wound," Dad said, trying to shake off the bollocking he knew was coming his way.

"Ronnie, it's not funny," Mum said. "Great example of gun safety to be showing the boys! Go inside and find a plaster or something." The anger was clear in her voice as she rushed over and put her arms around me, soaking herself as she comforted me. "Come on, sweetheart, let's go and find you a towel and get you dry. Robert, I think it's best you go home now, darling. Come back another day when the pool's warmer."

But he didn't. Robert probably thought Dad was a complete maniac, or maybe he told his parents what happened, and *they* stopped him from coming back. Whatever the reason, it took a good year before we started becoming best buddies again, and it stung – far more than the Blu Tack wound.

Despite the humiliation of that event, I forgave Dad, like I always do. He genuinely seemed so sorry afterwards and said he would make it up to me. He tried. He bought me the latest *Medal of Honour* game for the PlayStation, and a pair of Nike trainers I'd wanted, but he couldn't make up for the gap left in my life with Robert absent that summer.

Whilst other friends, and my cousins, came to use the pool, it was never quite as much fun. I missed Robert and the games of water tag we used to play. But the worse thing was that I don't think Dad even noticed. He revelled in telling everyone how I gave such a spectacular performance believing it was a genuine gunshot wound, what a bedraggled mess I had been, and how I was the first to test the temperature of the pool that year. But he never once asked why Robert wasn't hanging around that summer; he never checked in with me to see if I was okay with what happened that day.

I learnt early on not to question Dad. He had a scary temper, and it was his way or the highway. It's funny how negative memories stick in our mind, and one that often haunts me is the time I disobeyed him when he had confiscated my PlayStation. I'd lied to him about pinching his cigarettes, and he finally caught me one day down at the stables. He went ballistic, which I find hypocritical being as he smokes. He grabbed me by the hair and dragged me back up to the house where he called Mum to come and witness my castigation. She was disappointed, I know. She hates smoking and is always warning me not to go down the same path as Dad. But he roared like some fierce tiger, slamming his fist down on the table, making the potted plant vibrate. I just sat there, totally humiliated, and I promised I wouldn't do it again.

"It's not good enough, James, we've taught you better than this," he said. "Your PlayStation is off limits for the next month and let that be a lesson to you."

I can still feel that anger which seemed to twist his face into a hideous unnameable monster with flaring nostrils and bared teeth. I said nothing, and took my punishment… until a few weeks later when the summer holidays came and I was bored one day.

Mum was down at the stables, and had invited me to go with her, but I refused, avoiding the risk of being forced to get on the saddle and ride. Ever since the time Starlight galloped off with me and I fell, winding myself, I had developed an enormous aversion to horses. It was the most terrifying feeling, having the air crushed out of my lungs, and I thought in that one awful moment that I was going to die.

"The more you show him you're nervous, the more he'll play you up," Mum had said, when I told her he was being frisky and had bucked a short while earlier. But how could I not be nervous, sat up there on that huge black machine which was three times the size of me. The more she insisted he could sense my nerves, the more nervous I became. I was at the mercy of this great beast and counting the minutes until I could descend and be on firm ground again, back to safety.

Well, it didn't end well, and I hadn't expected to land back on the ground at quite such high speed. Rather than console me, Mum went tearing after Starlight, concerned that he would jump the fence and break free.

Stacey saw what happened from the stables and rushed to comfort me. I remember the embarrassment for displaying my upset so unashamedly, crying for Mum and feeling a sense of panic that she hadn't rushed to check if I was okay.

Fortunately, being as how Dad doesn't like horses either, he understood, and later that day he told Mum it was time to stop forcing me to ride and let me choose. I chose to never ride again, but I clearly remember the expression on Mum's face, as though she didn't quite believe me.

So, Mum was down at the stables, and Dad had gone off to meet some friend for golf (I don't know why, since he doesn't play golf) and there was nobody free to meet up with from school. I'd been kicking around the house all morning and decided to go and find my PlayStation from Dad's office. It didn't take me long to find it and I carefully removed it from the sideboard cabinet in his office, and crept to the TV room to plug it in.

I was mid-game when I heard the front door bang as it closed. Hoping it was the cleaner, I ventured out to the hallway, only to be met by Dad, who had decided to come home for lunch. He looked strangely unruffled, his hair perfectly groomed – apart from the one side of his fringe that always flops down, and not a bead of sweat on his beige polo top that matched the colour of his hair. Mum always says he looks like Don Johnson (whoever that is?) but the thing I tend to notice the most is his beady eyes that can either be full of mischief, or a dark seriousness that makes me nervous. They were giving off no warning signals that day.

"You're not supposed to be home until this afternoon," I said, trying to appear as normal as possible.

"I gave up on the fifth hole. Honestly, it doesn't matter how many times Charles tries to convince me, I hate the game. Too much walking and not enough action. I'm off out after lunch though. Are you alright?" He looked at me quizzically.

74

"Yeah, sure. Bit bored, but I'm okay," I lied. "Can I have lunch with you?" I was careful to keep my voice balanced and calm. If I could just get lunch over with and Dad out the door again, I could go back to my PlayStation with him none the wiser.

I planted myself down on a kitchen stool by the marble breakfast bar, whilst Dad flicked on the espresso maker. I couldn't gauge his mood. Nervously, I ran my finger along the scalloped edge of the brightly-coloured fruit bowl that Mum had brought back from Spain.

"I'm just having a cheese and pickle sandwich," Dad said, opening the fridge door to get out the ingredients. "Is that okay with you?"

"Sure, that's great."

Dad placed my sandwich down in front of me and headed for the door.

"Where are you going?" I asked, trying to hide my apprehension.

"To the toilet, is that okay?"

"Of course," I said, giving an embarrassed snigger.

When Dad returned, he asked about my day and I began to relax. It seemed he was in a good mood after all, and he was showing interest in me for a change.

"Not too bored then?"

I nibbled at my sandwich, not wanting to mention that he had put too much pickle in for my liking. "Well, I finished a new picture I've been working on, do you want to see it?" Whilst I lied, I did have a new piece of artwork burrowed in my art folder that he hadn't yet seen. I could show it to him if he wanted.

"No, son. Eat your sandwich," he replied, tucking into his. "Is that all you've been up to this morning?"

"Er, yeah, and reading comics," I said, which was true.

Then the explosion happened.

As if out of nowhere, his voice bellowed with rage, and he grabbed me by my arm and dragged me out of the kitchen. I knew exactly where he was taking me.

The PlayStation cables were spread across the TV room carpet, along with the discarded controls and my game paused on the huge fifty-inch screen.

"So, would you mind telling me what the hell this is?" Dad's eyes were bulging as if they were going to pop out on stalks and I felt his full disgust as though it were pushing through my pores.

I immediately began crying like a snivelling idiot, begging him for mercy and telling him how sorry I was. But I had disobeyed him and needed to be taught a lesson. He started to wallop me across my backside, and I jumped and dodged, trying to avoid the full brunt of his mighty hand.

He marched me to my bedroom by the scruff of my neck and threw me on the bed.

A short while later, he returned to see me after he had changed into what I called his 'dudeish gear'; a pair of cargo trousers with a black T-shirt and Converse trainers, that I would so want to borrow if he were my size. I thought for a moment that he had taken pity on me, that he was returning to make things right, but instead, he said that if I left my bedroom at any time other than for the toilet, he would know.

"I have eyes on the house," he said. Then he threatened that my PlayStation would be thrown in the bin should I disobey, and he would ban me from having any friends over for the remainder of the summer holidays.

He finally left, with just the sickening smell of his aftershave lingering, like his hallmark in the air, reminding me not to disobey. It fuelled my anger for him. I spent the rest of the day crying in my bedroom, wishing Max was there to console me, but he was down at the yard with Mum. The anger somehow swallowed up a part of me that afternoon, and a new skill emerged – the art of suppressing the humiliation and shame that consumed me all too often. It was as though I wrapped it all up and sealed it with shrink film before deliberately placing it into an imaginary box that I closed the lid on, and buried.

When Mum returned and asked me what I was doing in my bedroom, I chose not to tell her what had happened earlier. My face naturally learnt to follow the command from somewhere deep inside me and showed indifference. It worked; she seemed to have no suspicion that I'd been crying all afternoon. I knew she would have been angry with Dad, had I told her, but if she confronted him it would have made things a whole lot worse, so I kept my silence. If Dad told her, then that was up to him; she would hear *his* version of events and that was the way he would have wanted it.

It annoys me these days that Dad has a new way to target me, through Rachel. It annoys me even more how she takes his jokes in 'good spirit'.

"I don't know why you let him get to you," she said after the prank he played with Bella. "I'm over it, and if you think about it, nobody was hurt." But then, she hasn't had a lifetime of his pranking. She didn't grow up learning how to balance his childish laughter and acting as if he were my best pal one minute, with the disciplining father the next. Consequently, I loved him but also struggled with the guilt I had for not liking him.

Chapter 7

RONNIE

There's an abundance of energy in the air. The vibrant colours bordering the garden and the sun glinting on the tennis court awakens my senses. I love the spring. Everything seems to come alive, and there's the anticipation of lazy hot summer days relaxing by the pool, drinking a gin and tonic on the terrace and entertaining friends with barbecues.

Amanda was as keen to jump out of bed as me this morning. She downed her morning coffee at around seven and shot off to the stables after laying out my breakfast for me.

Martyn isn't due to arrive for another hour. It's our second tennis session this year, and we have a maximum of two hours to play, since he's promised Meghan that he'll take her shopping this afternoon. To fill the time, I sit at the breakfast bar flicking through some jokey feeds on Facebook, drinking a double espresso, when a clip catches my eye. It's perfect, and I have just the right tools to carry it out.

After fetching a box of matches from the firewood basket in the lounge, I return to the kitchen where I locate a pair of scissors from the cutlery drawer. I set about carefully beheading the matchsticks, binning the sticks, and putting the little red heads to one side. I'll have to be quick if I'm going to get this done before Martyn arrives.

The clock says 9.40 a.m. as I fetch a Stanley knife from my toolbox. I carefully slit one of my tennis balls open, just wide enough to fit the match heads in. Then, I carefully place each one through the hole until the ball is about three quarters full. The guy on Facebook covered the slit with duct tape, but that would give the game away, so I fetch the epoxy glue that Amanda bought last week to fix her Lladro ornament. It leaves a slight mark as it dries, but it won't notice once thrown in the basket with all the other balls. There's no doubt in my mind, that with the impact of one of Martyn's magnificent serves, the ball will explode, leaving him in a ball of smoke, just like the video.

After putting away the evidence, I hear Martyn's car on the drive. Perfect timing. I grab my tennis racket and place the prank ball in my bag along with my sports bottle and towel.

"You ready for a good thrashing then?" Martyn says, as I shut the front door.

As he locks his car, I notice how cool he looks in his aviator shades, his perfectly-ironed Lacoste polo top and white tennis shorts. It strikes me that he wears something

80

different every time we play, and I imagine he has a whole wardrobe, just for his sporting attire.

"In your dreams!" I reply. "Your chauffeur allowed the day off today?" I give him a friendly thump on the back.

"He never works at the weekend; besides, I'd forget how to drive."

Martyn opens the gate that leads round the back of the house and, as I follow him, I notice he's looking trim.

"You really are looking thinner, Skinner."

"Yeah, I decided it would help me to whip your ass on the court." His laugh makes me smile. It seems I'm not the only one with secret tactics to win. My private lessons have certainly made a difference, and I beat him three sets to one last week.

We stop off to pick up two baskets of tennis balls from the summer house and head for the court. I'm glad I have my tracksuit jacket on, as there's a nip in the air and the freshly cut grass is layered with dew. It's nearly time to take the cover off the pool, and I make a mental note to ask Amanda to book our gardener to come and give it a clean. It will be nice to have it open again; it looks like an empty ice-rink with its blue net acting as a canvas on the kidney-shaped pool, and somewhat lonely without the sun loungers that have been stored in the garage for winter.

Halfway across the lawn, I steer Martyn away from an unpleasant mess left by Daisy.

"God, I'm sorry, Martyn," I say.

It infuriates me if there is any dog mess in the garden. It's Amanda's job to clear it up and she knows I won't tolerate it being left. There is no need for it! Daisy gets plenty of walks, and practically lives down in the paddock with the horses; she should get all her business done down there.

"It's why I won't have a dog," Martyn says, as we reach the green wire fencing.

While I sit and tie my trainer laces on the wooden bench, Martyn goes to check the height of the net. Most people just use the height of a racket with another laid across the top, but no, Martyn likes to go the full hog and brings his own metal tape measure. It gives me the perfect opportunity to bury the prank tennis ball at the bottom of his basket, and I feel a jitter of excitement at the prospect of the shock he will receive if the ball explodes. The two videos I watched demonstrated the tennis ball being thrown against a wall, and a cloud of smoke igniting like a dud firework, nothing too dramatic, and I'm more than confident that it's safe.

With our warm-up finished, and after a couple of practice serves, I suggest we get going with our match. I don't want Martyn to reach the prank ball before we're well into the game, so we spin the racket for who serves first. It's me.

Fire surges through my body. I feel so powerful, so unstoppable as I thrust down with my serve. The vibration of my racquet makes the fire burn hotter and the first set gets off to an intense start.

By the end of the second game, the sweat drips down my face, but I hardly notice. It's one game all and my serve again. If only Martyn would stop picking up balls, and use the damn balls in his basket, the prank can claim its glory. I'm beyond eager to see whether it works or not.

Slicing a drop shot at forty-thirty, I take the third game and we both head to the bench for a breather. We usually change ends, but I need to convince him otherwise, since I'll end up with his basket of balls on his side. Not something I had thought through.

"So, James is doing well," Martyn says.

"Not today, Martyn. No business talk on the tennis court, remember?"

"I wasn't talking about work, I meant generally, you know."

"Oh yeah, of course. Sorry. They've decided to postpone the wedding plans to next year for some reason, probably too much to organise in such a short time," I say, trying to make up for my snappy remark, "but they seem happy in their new home... they're saving up for a new bathroom since they won't let me pay for it."

Well, they took my fifty thousand pound deposit quite happily, but I imagine Rachel feels a tad embarrassed and wants to feel the reward of doing the place up with their own earnings.

"Never seen my boy so happy," I add. "I really think he's going places."

After returning my drink to the bag, I head off to my end of the court again.

"Not changing ends then?" Martyn says.

"Can if you want," I bluff, "but the sun's equal at both ends."

"Okay, I'm happy if you are."

The game is forty/fifteen to Martyn, and he has two balls left in his basket. I know one of them is the prank ball and I position myself to receive his serve, my sway slightly exaggerated with anticipation of what could be about to happen.

I watch as he stretches to reach the ball; his feet lift off the ground as he smashes it towards my forearm. I circle my arm back ready to receive it, but just as the ball hits the ground in front of me, it erupts into a ball of sparks like a firework. The flame that erupts forces me backwards and I land square on my arse. I'm left in a cloud of smoke as Martyn runs towards me.

"Christ, what was that?" he says. I choke on the stench of sulphur, and he reaches for my hand to help pull me up.

"A joke on me," I reply, spluttering.

Martyn's face erupts into a smile. "You've singed your eyebrows," he says, trying not to laugh.

I'm mortified. Not only was it a slightly more dangerous trick than I had imagined, it backfired on me big time.

"What were you thinking? That could have exploded in your face!" Martyn says, clearly annoyed at my latest prank.

"Yeah, well, it did, kind of. Only it was supposed to be yours," I say.

"Thanks!"

"No, in the video it just burst into smoke, there was no flame that came out of it. That was like a bloody exploding Roman candle. Perhaps I put too many match ends in the ball."

"You did what?" Martyn's bemused face makes me laugh.

"Yep, saw it on a Facebook video and thought it would be good for a laugh."

"You are intolerable sometimes, Ron! One of these days you're gonna give someone a heart attack or something."

He has a point. That nearly scared the shit out of me. In that split second while I focused on the ball, it never occurred to me that it was going to explode on my side of the net, and make me jump as if I hadn't been in on the joke. I'm disappointed that I didn't think quickly enough to deny any knowledge of the deed. I reckon Martyn would have taken quite some time to realise that I was the culprit who had created the mysterious exploding tennis ball.

The match over at two sets to one, we head back in silence, each of us with the metal ball carriers slung over our shoulders. I'm sweating as if it's a blazing hot day, but the damp patio furniture tells me the sun still hasn't heated up to any great degree.

"Well, victory all round. Same time next week – weather permitting?" Martyn says.

I can barely contain my frustration as I light a cigarette.

"Yep, sure. That stupid prank of mine really set me back. I think I pulled a muscle in my lower back when I fell," I say, with little more than a bruised ego at losing, and a possible bruised buttock cheek. But I'm angry. I don't like losing, and I like it even less if my opponent rubs my nose in it.

"Text me with a time for a meeting next week, I have a few ideas for Back Up Security that I want to run by you," I say. Martyn nods as he opens his car door.

After seeing Martyn off, I text Amanda down at the stables. *Are you down there all afternoon?* I'm secretly hoping for her answer to be yes, meaning I can message Penny and see if I can pop over to hers. I'm not in a good mood after the prank misfired and I need to release my stress with some great sex.

Got a pack-up lunch. Girls coming over to help me paint the stable doors after mucking out the barn. I'm just cleaning and conditioning the tack then riding Starlight. X

Good, just the answer I was hoping for.

I text Penny, who obliges with a *Yes I'm free.* My excitement and energy resurface as I head for the shower. It's just what I need right now. Someone to massage my ego a little and make me feel special. I have an intense fear of failure, something I am well aware of. I guess it stems from childhood; most things do.

My father was always detached, leaving Mum to do all the child-rearing. He spent every available hour of the day working, while she ran the home and brought up me and my sister. He had worked his way up the ladder with a well-known department store, starting out selling electrical goods in his teens, and ending up as store manager. But Mum had an endless appetite for the finer things in life, so he took on part-time shifts working for a local taxi firm. It was the fact that he was never around, and always complaining about the people he worked for, that made me decide from a young age that I would be self-employed. Also, the fact that despite providing a decent income which fed Mum's endless desire for indulgent shopping sprees, he was never around to enjoy the money himself. As fast as he earned it, she spent it. No, I wanted to earn *a lot* of money. Money that I could enjoy spending, and be around to enjoy with my family – should I have one.

I was constantly pressured by my mother nagging me to do well and not 'waste' my education. This bothered me more than the rejection of being sent away, whilst my sister got to stay at home.

"Make us proud," she would say as she uncurled my fingers that refused to let go of her coat on the first day of term. Other mothers had watery eyes with their farewells, but not mine. Mum could turn on the tears when she wanted – mid-fight with Dad – but she was probably worried it would smudge her perfectly applied mascara in front of the other parents.

I don't recall much fun or laughter in the home. When Dad was about, there were blazing rows and he would slate my mum with words I had never even heard of. He would criticise her for not doing things the way he wanted, and not having us in bed when he got home. It wasn't a pleasant atmosphere, so it made no sense that I would continually try to escape from the boarding school I was sent to.

The *worst* part of my childhood was boarding school. The disempowerment was soul-destroying. In the early days, I didn't know how to verbalise to my parents about the bullying, or the loneliness that I felt. There were tears, and my begging not to go back, but both my parents mostly ignored this or reminded me that they were paying good money for my education, and that I needed to learn to start showing my appreciation.

Each time I tried to run away, I was swiftly returned by Dad, shamed and told that I was letting him and my mother down. As time progressed, I realised that I had no choice but to accept my lot. This was confirmed when Mum wrote a letter to the head to say that she had some concerns after my tooth was broken, but I was called to his office and made to bend over his desk for ten blows from his cane. What's more, if any of the sixth-formers caught wind that there had been a complaint, they would come and beat you up for being a snitch and make the following term a living hell.

I harboured great resentment towards my dad for many years, and regret that I never told him just how bad it was at school, since I'll never get the chance now. He's been gone five years. He died of a severe stroke which happened in the middle of a blazing row with Mum – nothing out of the ordinary there. Apparently, he just fell on the spot, and was dead before the ambulance arrived. A blessing that it was quick, and I don't think he suffered.

Mum was left to play the grieving widow but I know she's catching up on all the things she always wanted to pursue. Bridge clubs, W.I. meetings and singing in the choir at church. She has a hectic social life these days, which lessens the burden that I don't get up to visit her in Norfolk as often as I should. My sister Sandra only lives an hour away from her, and it's more down to the daughter to stay in touch anyway.

I put on my faded jeans with a plain grey Tom Ford T-shirt. I spritz some Paco Rabanne on my neck and three-day stubble beard before grabbing my black jacket and heading for the door.

The sun hits my face as I skip down the front steps. Bees are humming around the lavender pots, and I feel the buzz of summer looming.

My mojo is back. Life is good.

Chapter 8

JAMES

My stomach is doing somersaults as I walk into Lucas Wilson's consulting room. I promised Rachel that I would see a counsellor to help with my anxiety and low moods, and Mum sought out this guy for me who apparently specialises in psychodynamic therapy with young adults. I'm reluctant, since the counselling I had some years back was a complete waste of time. But I wear my best poker face to try and disguise the *I'm here because I've been told I have to be* look.

"Take a seat," Lucas says, pointing towards one of the two brown high-back chairs by the window.

I sit down with my arms firmly crossed, shifting my eyes around to scan the room. The coffee table between us, the casually placed potted plants and the turquoise seascape picture hanging above his chair make a poor attempt to create a homely atmosphere. I'm not here for afternoon tea and cake or a friendly catch-up on the latest episode of *Game of Thrones*. I'm here to have my headspace invaded, which will, no doubt, be as painful as gouging my brain out with a dessert spoon.

"So, what brings you to me today?" Lucas asks.

"Er, to get rid of my headaches hopefully," I reply, realising that I could just as easily have seen a regular GP for this. "And I've been having some nightmares recently."

"Well, there's no rush here, James. Your mother has said she is happy to pay for these sessions for ten weeks, and then to reassess whether you want any more."

What the hell?

Mum and Rachel may well have discussed me having some therapy, which I've agreed to on the condition they don't mention it to Dad, but I had no idea Mum thinks it necessary to have ten sessions; I presumed two or three would be enough to get them both off my back.

My muscles stiffen as I begin to bite the edge of my fingernail and I find I cannot look Lucas in the eye. It's as if these psychologists can see straight into your soul through your eyes, and whilst I don't have anything to hide, I feel nervous about this stranger probing into my thoughts. I stare at the faded coffee cup ring that marks the table between us.

"Why don't we start by talking about what is making you anxious," he says, leaning back into his chair as though settling in for a long, cosy story, which I am *not* about to give him.

"Er, being here to talk to a strange man that I don't know from Adam," I reply.

Lucas laughs. "Of course, it will feel weird at first, but I can assure you, anything we chat about is kept safely

91

within these walls. I only have this notebook to remind myself of any details that may be useful when we talk again in our next session." He pats the navy-blue notebook that is, as yet, unopened on his lap.

"Can I get you a drink, James?" He points to the sideboard on which is a tray with two cups and little sachets of coffee and tea bags, like you find in a hotel room. Will I be rewarded with a pack of two-finger shortbread if I begin talking? I wonder.

"A coffee would be great," I say, stretching my hands to try and release the tension from them.

They say a watched kettle never boils, well, after Lucas sits back down in front of me, the interminable silence doesn't lift. We sit listening intently to the hot water make its crescendo in the shiny pint-sized kettle. I'm reluctant to speak, since I know how these counsellors always delve into your childhood, and I'm more than aware of mine, warts and all, and do not want it all trawled up and psychoanalysed. It's the present day I'm interested in, and the future. The one with Rachel becoming my wife and having children running around our home.

"I think they may have started when I got my recent promotion at work," I say.

"The headaches?" Lucas asks. *Oh God, has it been that long since he asked the question?*

He places a mug of steaming black coffee in front of me on a white ceramic coaster and I begin to crave a cigarette.

"Yes, er no. I mean the nightmares."

"And how do you feel about the promotion?"

Here we go. The quintessential counsellor question, *'And how does that make you feel?'*

I'm suddenly aware of my defensive body language, which is in stark contrast to Lucas who is now comfortably nestled in his chair as though settling in for a night watching TV; all he needs is a pair of comfy PJs, a mug of hot chocolate and a remote in his hand instead of a pen. I attempt to mirror him and sit my butt deeper in the back of the chair, placing my back against the soft leather backrest and placing one hand on each knee. I must look as though I'm preparing for take-off. All I need is the picture on the wall behind Lucas to flash a red seat-belt sign and I'd half expect an air hostess to arrive with her drinks trolley and a much-needed vodka and tonic. I remove my hands from my knees and clasp them together.

For reasons unknown to me, I start to open up a little. I explain how I'm not happy at work, and how I hide this from everyone. Lucas reacts with genuine interest, absorbing every word with a warm smile fixed to his face and a kindness in his eyes that are full of patience and understanding. Feeling encouraged, I slowly peel away the tough outer layer that protects me like the papery brown skin of an onion and am surprised at how easily the words begin to flow.

"That's your hour up, I'm afraid," Lucas says, which jolts my senses like my early morning alarm call. It immediately brings me back to my surroundings, as though the lights have just come up in the cinema to signal the film is over and it's time to leave. I glance at the oversized clock on the wall, imagining it melting like the Dali picture. It's bang on the hour.

"But we will carry on where you've left off next week, James," he says.

After I leave Lucas's office, I'm surprised by the spring in my step as I head off up the high street. The lightness I feel makes me think of the film *The Green Mile,* and how John Coffey would suck the badness or disease out of characters before coughing the magical particles out into the atmosphere, leaving himself drained in the process. I'm immediately guilt-ridden, wondering if I have drained Lucas; what would he do to relieve himself of the negative crap that has just emanated from my mouth and infiltrated his thoughts?

I begin to counteract my guilt-ridden thoughts of overburdening Lucas with the thought of how much Mum is probably paying him. His friendly warm face starts to fade, and I think of him in the cold light of day for what he is – a psychotherapist. It's his job.

Chapter 9

RONNIE

The hibiscus notes of an espresso filtrate my senses as I enter the kitchen. Amanda has laid out the table, with my daily Weetabix in a porcelain bowl waiting for the full-fat milk from the dainty little Port Merion jug her mother gifted us.

"Do you want a fry-up this morning?" Amanda asks, bringing my espresso to the table.

She's kitted out in her jodhpurs and a scruffy fleece top that hugs to her slender body. She's not what I would exactly describe as sexy. Her hair is in its mandatory thick braid, hanging down her back with over bleached dry-ends fanned around the bottom of a scrunchie. Her face is still youthful, but I wish she would wear a little light makeup – something to make her a little more feminine. I'm being harsh though; she is pretty, and her figure, whilst quite flat-chested, is one many women her age would admire.

"No thanks, darling. I'll just have some toast and marmalade today," I reply, as I reach for the *Daily Mail* lying in the middle of the stained oak table. Amanda makes the most amazing homemade marmalade, and slathered onto fresh thick wholemeal toast, it is just the best.

Amanda grabs her smoothie and joins me. She's on one of her 'health-kicks' again, and the green sludge looks like something she's drained from the bottom of a swamp.

"I don't know how you drink that stuff," I say. 'It looks like you've liquidised Kermit the Frog."

"It's delicious, the fresh pineapple disguises the taste of spinach and kale," she replies. "You should try it. It would help get off those extra few pounds you keep moaning about."

She's right, I'm not happy with the surplus weight I've gained. My trousers are all starting to feel too tight, and I have to disguise the slight muffin top that's appearing over my belt-line. We have a home gym that we built an extension for and I work out in it most mornings. Admittedly I don't use the running machine much anymore, but I cycle on the exercise bike for fifteen to twenty minutes every day, and use the bench for sit-ups. My tennis is good for keeping fit too, although only when I play somebody who's my level so they get me running around the court. But, despite my regular exercise, it seems that this middle-age spread isn't a myth after all. The midnight snacks and sneaky visits to the fridge when I can't sleep need to stop.

"Point taken," I say, "but there must be a better way than drinking that shit."

Amanda ignores my response. "Don't forget to put our trip to Malaga in your diary. I've booked the kennels and flights."

"Oh, yes. Thanks, love. When is it again?"

"Last two weeks of June, before the kids break up for summer holidays," she says.

Lorraine and Ray are our best friends. We make a point of going out to their pad in Malaga once a year. Their kids grew up with James who is now best friends with their son Dan. Their daughter Kiera was always such a sweet little thing – all frocks and frills as a child, although a little sensitive, a typical trait of girls, I guess. One advantage of not having a daughter is there's less to worry about. Kiera is all grown up these days, wearing short leather skirts and skimpy tops, and I find myself strangely protective of her. I even said to Ray that I was surprised he lets her out wearing what seems nothing more than a belt around her thighs. He just shrugged and said that it wasn't worth sweating the small stuff, in his usual laid-back manner.

Ray and I go back to childhood. He was the one person I trusted at boarding school, and he would always come and share his tuck box with me, or leave little notes under my pillow when he knew I felt sad. We've never talked about the bullying that went on, and I'm not sure if he got his fair share like me, since it's been buried in a vault of forgotten memories that neither of us ever bring up in the present.

By some fluke, we met our respective wives at the same time, in fact, we tossed a coin to see who would chat up which of the two when we spotted Lorraine and Amanda at the local disco (something neither of them know to this day). I have no regrets, since it's easy being married to Amanda, whereas Ray often complains that Lorraine is high maintenance, both emotionally and financially.

They split up for a period while Lorraine was in her late teens and Amanda and I were up to our eyes in nappies, before reuniting and tying the knot a couple of years later. If I'm honest, I was jealous of those few years where Ray sowed his wild oats and was seemingly shagging everything in a skirt. Amanda was only the third girl I had slept with, and I had hoped for a little more 'life' experience before settling down, but it wasn't her fault the condom split. It was neither of ours. What are the odds that the one time that should happen she would fall pregnant?

Amanda was only seventeen and a virgin when we met. Despite the fact her parents weren't overly strict and would no doubt support her, she was petrified when she discovered she was pregnant. I was in my early twenties and had had no thoughts of marriage, but did the honourable thing and married her when she was around five months pregnant. My parents were not impressed, so to avoid any arguments, we sneaked off to the registry office with Lorraine and Ray as witnesses. I have no regrets though, she keeps me on the straight and narrow, and is a wonderful mother to our son.

"And, don't forget Barbados the first two weeks of October," Amanda says excitedly. I nod and smile to acknowledge that I've heard her before contemplating what we'll get up to this year in Malaga. James and Rachel won't be joining us, which is a shame, but they're too engrossed in doing up their new place.

Last year was Rachel's first time to Malaga with us, and James was much more relaxed on the flight having her sat next to him. He's never been great with flying, but then he's like me, scared of crashing. There's something very intimidating about being thirty thousand feet up in the air at the mercy of the skies with the pilot at the yoke. I never feel more out of control than on a flight and need a few gin and tonics to calm my nerves.

Daisy, our chocolate Lab, comes sniffing round my ankles for crumbs. Amanda doesn't agree with feeding titbits from the table, but I secretly drop a crust on the floor which she swallows in one gulp. She looks up at me with her pink-rimmed eyes to say thank you, but then I turn away when she tilts her head as if asking for more.

Amanda is clearing away the breakfast things when our cleaner, Chrissie, arrives.

"Don't worry about those Mrs T, I'll clear breakfast,' she says, relieving Amanda of the plates in her hand. I love how she calls us Mr and Mrs T, like the big guy from the A-Team.

It's only Amanda and me in the house these days, but we still need Chrissie – so Amanda insists. Whilst we don't have the aftermath of James's teenage shenanigans or his trail of dirty crockery to clear up anymore, it's a big place to keep on top of. I suppose she's right – we have got five bedrooms, all with ensuites, and downstairs, we have the gym extension along with five other living spaces which includes the kitchen/breakfast room.

I love my home. Whilst not in the palatial league that some company directors live in, this home has character and has been a great party-house over the years. It saddens me how quiet it is nowadays though, other than our old faithfuls coming round for meals now and again, or James and Rachel visiting us, it feels like the life has gone from it. I would like nothing more than to fill it with grandchildren, perhaps even hold their birthday parties here one day.

So, whilst the house only needs a flick over with a duster, I don't begrudge Amanda having a cleaner, despite her not bringing in an income. It was mainly my decision after having James that she didn't look for work. It took quite some time for her to recover from the caesarean due to an infection, and she was kept up most nights in the first year of James's life. She was never happy in her work anyway, her choices limited by so few qualifications which meant she went from washing hair in salons to being a cashier at Tesco's, where she was working when I met her.

Mum and Dad were total snobs, and made it clear that a checkout girl was not the sort of girl they imagined me ending up with. But we had a connection and I *did* love her. I think she sees me as the white knight who rescued her from a life of potential drudgery, as money certainly gives the freedom of choices in life.

There was no point in harbouring regrets with the unplanned pregnancy and, as it turns out, it was the best thing that ever happened to me – to '*us*'. Back Up was starting to take shape, and thankfully, I was able to support the both of us. My parents learnt to accept my choice – eventually. I think it helped that we provided their first grandson, and Mum clearly approved that Amanda chose to be a stay-at-home mother like she did. That's where the similarity ends though; Amanda has never been a big spender, and holds on to her integral childhood values with 'waste not, spend not' her default setting.

I'm well looked after, Amanda is great at running the home and keeping on top of maintenance (which she tells me is like painting the Forth Bridge), and she takes care of all the laundry and meals too. She's always been there for James, often filling the space for both us at his school plays or football matches. She's a loyal, loving individual, so she more than deserves a little help around the home to free up time to attend to her beloved horses. It keeps her happy and fulfils her childhood dreams, which makes me happy.

"What are you up to today?" Amanda asks, grabbing her Barbour jacket from the back of the chair. It's Saturday, a day that we rarely spend together.

"Oh, nothing much – meeting Martyn and Ray down at the Lodge to sort out the next stage," I reply convincingly.

The Lodge is a development of cottages that Martyn and I recently invested in, with Ray project managing the renovations. I like to keep my hand in a variety of different things, and you can't keep me away from a good business investment. We should double our money by the time we come to sell, and whilst Ray hasn't invested as much as us, he'll take a fifty percent cut of the profit since he's overseeing it all.

Amanda kisses me tenderly on the cheek as we stand on the front porch. "Love you, Ron. Have a good day and stay out of trouble!"

I laugh as she heads off towards the paddock. "Love you too, Mandy." She hates me calling her Mandy, but I do it sometimes just to annoy her.

The Aston crunches on the gravel as I slowly pull out of our horseshoe driveway. I call Penny as I know she should be free on a Saturday. Martyn and Ray know to cover for me should Amanda speak to their wives, as they're both in on my plans for today. The little white lie I told Amanda was for a very good reason. It's her fortieth birthday coming up and I have a wonderful surprise in store.

As well as being the master of all jokes, I also pride myself on being the master of wonderful surprises. Amanda and I haven't had a party in years; we used to be quite the socialites with our two-yearly extravaganzas, but they have fallen by the wayside, so her fortieth is the perfect opportunity for a big celebration, and I want to make sure that she knows nothing about it.

Penny sent out the invites for me, with a list of instructions where everybody should park, what time to arrive etc and today I plan to buy some decorations and a couple of small gifts to give Amanda on the morning so that she doesn't suspect anything. Then, mid-party, she'll be receiving my best surprise of all… a German Shepherd puppy. It's been seven months since we lost Max, and there's signs she's ready for another one now. Martyn and Meghan are picking it up the day before her birthday and I've asked them to source a box big enough that we can present it to her like one of those magical scenes from a Disney movie.

Penny picks up.

"Hi, sweetheart, fancy meeting me for some shopping?" I ask.

"I'm busy this morning, Ronnie." Penny's soft voice is on loudspeaker. I feel my stomach dip. If only I had planned things a bit better, sent her a text last night, but I'm reluctant to start messaging her from home. Our affair is only successful so long as I don't slip into dangerous habits and I make it a rule to never message her from home, and she knows if I don't reply to her messages then that is where I am.

"I could meet you for lunch though?" she adds. "How about a ploughman's at the pub?"

I smile. "Perfect, I'll see you at The Black Horse at one-thirty." I secretly hope to get all my shopping done beforehand, so that I can slip back to hers after we finish lunch.

"Don't be late," Penny says.

I sip my gin and slimline tonic in a quiet corner tucked around the back of the pub. Whilst I know the staff from Back Up tend to use the fancier wine bars in the next street it's not beyond the realms of possibility someone could frequent this place – even at the weekend.

My trusty leather Filofax beckons, and I enter the dates of our June trip to Malaga before it slips my mind. Our Caribbean holiday is a little late this year, but two weeks in Barbados sounds like bliss. Whilst I'm not a vain person I do so love getting a golden glow from the sun. There's nothing quite like that glorious tingle at the end of a day when you slather on the after-sun and feel revitalised by all that vitamin D. To top it off, Amanda is usually up for sex when we're away, so I'm thoroughly spoilt with the quintessential sea, sex, and sun.

Hopefully, Amanda's booked first-class. She knows I like plenty of leg room and there's nothing worse than a nine-hour flight packed in like sardines, with someone's kid poking you in the back. I'm a nervous passenger, and find small things grate on my nerves: getting stuck behind the drinks trolley, waiting in the queue for the toilet, and noisy kids – these things irritate me to the point of silent fury causing me to give a death stare which never improves things.

Once we're airborne I'm fine, so long as there's no turbulence. I get my head into a good book and put my headphones on to block out the noise, including Amanda's constant attempts to chatter. I've told her more than once that I don't want to talk when we fly.

I've never played a prank on a flight, but that doesn't stop me fantasising about it. It's a good job I'm not a pilot. The little devil on my shoulder always gives me the same thought when flying: if I were the pilot, I would simply *have* to have a little fun with the passengers. I'd make an announcement over the tannoy.

"Ladies and gentlemen, this is your captain speaking. Would you please fasten your seatbelts in preparation for my final manoeuvre before landing. It's something they said could never be done in a jumbo jet – a single barrel roll followed by a loop the loop!"

I would then bank the plane steeply to the left before straightening up. "Only kidding, we are now preparing for our descent into Heathrow Airport." It would certainly freak them all out for a few seconds, especially if they were nervous passengers like me.

Penny's arrival disturbs my thoughts.

"What did you buy?" she asks, kissing my ear and nibbling it. She knows all my weak spots.

"Oh, just a few bits for the party," I reply, not wanting to reveal how I've just bought a stunning tri-colour gold diamond necklace.

Amanda isn't big on jewellery – unlike Penny. I'm not even sure whether she's a gold or silver person, so opted for the safety of three-colour gold to cover all bases. It has a dainty heart-shaped pendant with a tiny solitaire diamond, and is far less than I would normally spend on her, only setting me back £850. The party is costing a small fortune though, and when Amanda meets the pup, I know she's going to be ecstatic. He didn't come cheap either; I got him from the same breeder where we got Max from, so, I know the pedigree has a good bloodline, and will be worth the price.

I move the shopping bags from the spare seat and place them on the floor under the table.

"Everything set for the party?" Penny asks, taking a sip from her glass.

"Pretty much," I reply, feeling slightly guilty that Penny isn't coming. She knows I prefer to keep her separate from my home life.

The only time Amanda has ever caught sight of her was at a work party she insisted on coming to last year. There were enough people there that Penny blended into the background, and despite me catching her look our way a couple of times, she kept herself perfectly out of sight.

"Who was the woman with the reddish hair in the gold dress?" Amanda asked on the way home. I don't

106

know how she picked up on her, since Penny hadn't come over to introduce herself. But then women notice other attractive women in the room and Penny had looked stunning in a gold one-shouldered full-length dress.

"Oh, do you mean Penny? She took Andreas's place as PA a while ago," I replied, nonchalantly.

"Oh, strange you didn't introduce us," she said, and I made my excuses, pretending I didn't know her very well.

Penny looks delicious as always, just one look from her green eyes has me grinning from ear to ear.

"The dog is being picked up by Martyn next week," she says. "A few days earlier than planned, but apparently his wife is pretty excited and Martyn hopes it doesn't give her any ideas. Amanda is going to die when she sees it!"

I feel equally guilty involving Penny in the preparations, but she's always so obliging. Never makes a fuss about these things, and I thank my lucky stars that she's content to have what little of me she can.

"Shall we order?" I ask, feeling my stomach grumbling.

Penny reaches for the menu on the table, and I catch a glimpse of the beautiful Cartier bracelet on her dainty wrist.

"Is the bracelet a little large for you?" I ask, reaching for her hand as I admire the panther snaking around her smooth pale skin.

"No, it's fine, Ronnie. I love it." Her eyes light up as she smiles, a childish glint of excitement in her eyes. "It's perfect."

As I put my knife and fork down on my empty plate, my phone buzzes, it's a message from James. Penny takes this as her cue to visit the powder room.

Hiya pops, we thought we would pop over and see you and Mum this afternoon. Are you about?

Shit! I hate lying. But I can't let Penny down again, there's only so many excuses I can make until she starts to get annoyed with me. Who am I kidding? It's *me* who can't handle the let-down. I've had an exhausting morning and been itching to see Penny the whole time I was shopping. There's no way I'm going to sacrifice an afternoon of delicious sex when I can easily postpone my son.

Hiya, James, tied up with meetings this afternoon, but why don't you both come over this evening? We can all get a takeaway and watch a film.

James responds immediately. *Coolio. See you both later. Xx*

I love my son. I love being a father. He keeps me young, and whilst I can't keep up with the lingo these days (my bad, your bad, what's that all about?) I consider myself quite a cool dad. It was difficult adapting to him growing up, and I'm probably guilty of being overly strict at times, but kids must learn respect. If they haven't got that, they aren't going to get very far in life.

There was no guidebook for parenting, but Amanda and I have done our best. We gave him the best education money could buy up until his GCSEs, which he flew through, but then things went a little downhill once he went to sixth form. It's only natural that he wanted to explore life, I suppose, but I can't pretend I wasn't a little disappointed that he didn't make it to uni. I tried not to make a big deal about it since James can be rather sensitive at times. Amanda calls it his 'mental health' but then we all have that, don't we? Yes, he lacks a certain confidence, but he's young, and I'm convinced working with the business is doing him the world of good; he has found his niche and is playing to his strengths. It's boosting his ego no end, especially now he's in a managerial role.

I text Amanda to tell her that I'll be home around five and that the kids are coming over for a takeaway. She'll be made up.

Penny wanders back from the powder room, her hair freshly brushed, and I take in her figure. Her short navy pinafore dress is elegant but understated, with black stockings and shoes that are a little too clunky for my liking. The collar on her white blouse has a 'choir boy' feel about it, and whilst it's not her usual kind of look, there is something rather pure and innocent about it that, rightly or wrongly, turns me on. I picture the black lace underwear she's probably wearing underneath and imagine her soft smooth curves, and tight firm breasts. I decide it's time for dessert.

"I'll get the bill, sweetheart," I say. "Back to yours for coffee?"

Chapter 10

JAMES

The more my father bangs on about how well I'm doing, how I'm going to take over the business as managing director one day, the more I feel trapped up a one-way street. I can't even tell Rachel how I truly feel, since she has this wholesome picture in her mind of four children seated around the table, with dogs and cats added to the mix, and all of us having the ideal holiday abroad once a year. I'm on such a good wage for my age, which Dad has clearly made possible, and it would shatter the whole picture if I stepped away to look at doing something else now. My future would become unknown.

If I could have chosen any career that I wanted, I think it would have been something in design. I always loved graphic design and art at school, and I was bloody good at it, even if I do say so myself. Some of my drawings had a 'disturbing nature' according to my school report, but they were good nonetheless.

My drawing of a gaunt Grim Reaper's head won the art prize in year six. It was a haunting, skeletal face carefully shaded in with one bulging eye threatening to pop out of the socket, and the other a deformed closed eyelid that hinted the eye was missing. The oversized mouth was sketched in a twisted grin like the Joker from Batman, revealing huge crooked teeth that were clenched together. But the best part was the hat. The haunted face was topped with a misshapen rumpled hat with three tentacles that hung down making it look like a jester's cap. It took me hours to get all the creases and lines shaded perfectly on the antique parchment paper that gave it just the right effect.

But, despite my art teachers trying to convince Mum and Dad that I should pursue art, it was never a choice. Everything is about money and success with Dad, and unless you're James Dyson or Monet, *there is no money to be had in the design or art world*, he would say, *far better to get a business degree behind you, and learn how large organisations work, it will give far wider scope for career choices.*

So, having deliberately flunked my A-levels to avoid having to do a business degree, I am a victim of my own failure. I should have been brave enough to fight for what I wanted to do. I should have fought to study art or design, since a career in design now would mean going back to square one. I would have to take on further study and an apprenticeship, and a low wage whilst I gain experience, and that isn't what Rachel has come to expect of me. It's okay for her, she loves teaching – it must be in the blood since she has seamlessly stepped into her mother's choice of career which makes her happy and, more annoyingly, fulfilled. Yes, I'm slightly envious that she is following a career of her choice, but even more so, a career that she enjoys.

Whilst I don't like working with Back Up, I do try every day to convince Rachel otherwise, since I'm just as keen to settle down with a family as she is, and like her, I would like as many children as possible. There is no way I would only want one child, having experienced the solitude of being an only child myself. I want my son or daughter to learn compassion and sharing from a young age; I want them to have the comfort of each other to turn to with problems in life and, most of all, to protect each other. There's always safety in numbers.

I'm convinced if I spend more time with Dad, I may find an opportunity one day to express how I feel about my career, but last night was certainly not that opportunity. Dad went to collect the two extra-large pizzas we had ordered, and he thought it would be funny to also order two extra small ones to wind us all up a little. I still can't believe that he went so far as to get a couple of empty large pizza boxes to put them in.

"These aren't extra-large," I said, wondering why the edges didn't touch the sides of the box when he opened them.

"Well, they're what you ordered," he said, having phoned from his car en route to order two small ones for his ridiculous prank. "I'm sure with some salad we can stretch them out between us." There wasn't a hint of a smirk on his face.

Mum joined us at the table with a bottle of wine and four glasses. Her face screwed up with confusion. "Ronnie, these aren't extra-large, you must have picked up the wrong order."

Dad picked up the boxes to examine them. "Nope, these definitely say extra-large," he said, "and that looks like pepperoni and this one is a meat feast."

Rachel gave me a quizzical look and started giggling.

"What?" I said, feeling the agitation begin to rise.

"Well, it's obvious, isn't it?"

"What's obvious?"

"Your dad's playing one of his jokes."

Dad maintained his poker face as if he had no idea what Rachel was implying.

"For God's sake, Dad, are you fooling around again?"

"Just eat the pizza, James, it looks delicious." He grabbed a tiny slice from the oversized box and placed it on his plate. A bubble of anxiety formed a knot in my stomach.

"No! I'll go down to the fucking pizza place and sort this out myself," I said, the hunger in my stomach increasing my rage.

I stood up to grab my car keys, with Mum rushing to my side to calm me down. At this point, Dad stood up. He calmly walked out of the house, went to his car, and returned with another two full-sized pizza boxes, this time with full-sized pizzas in.

"You got us," Rachel said, laughing at Dad who was annoyingly smug as we all sat back down to start our meal.

He shot me a look that said *learn to take a joke, son,* but I was so pissed off. Why the hell can't he just act like a grown up sometimes? He made me look a right jerk by making me so angry over a pizza and I just wasn't in the mood. I remained quiet throughout the meal and decided not to drink so that Rachel and I could go home afterwards. I couldn't bear how blasé Dad was about the whole thing; he has no idea how his tedious jokes, whether large or small, can have an adverse effect on people at times. We aren't always in a jolly mood for them.

My patience for Dad's practical jokes reached its limit after our last skiing holiday, which was in 2008. I was sixteen at the time and we went to the French alps with Martyn and Ray – a boys' holiday, where I was supposedly the only child in the party.

The four of us rented a luxury chalet in Val Thorens and Dad employed a chalet girl to cook and clean for us during our stay. There were the usual pranks played on the poor unsuspecting French girl, who took them in good spirit – mostly.

We were too exhausted at the end of the day to partake in much après ski, so would spend our evenings in the chalet playing cards around the table with a roaring log fire and copious amounts of Glühwein, whilst

Chantelle prepared our evening meal. All three of us played along with the hidden fart machine that Dad had placed in the under-sink cupboard, and every time he pressed the button we would look at the unsuspecting Chantelle, who was quite a bit older than me, and she would be blushing. She'd say in her pidgin English, "*Excusez-moi, messieurs*, it was not me," and we would return to our hand of pontoon pretending that we were slightly disgusted. We couldn't help but burst out laughing when she started to cough, trying to disguise the farting noise that relentlessly emanated from her direction.

Then, Chantelle was fed the obligatory hard-boiled egg prank one breakfast, sufficiently baffled as to why the egg was already cooked and throwing it in the bin before reaching for another one. Dad basked in his schoolboy glory and his friends united in his puerile humour, which forced me to join in. But that holiday was one where I realised I would no longer take his jokes in the same spirit I had as a child. It would no longer be enough to hear his apology and promise of some compensatory gift. I would no longer want to be the brunt of his annoying and humiliating jokes…

We were out on the slopes on a particularly glorious day. I'm at my most confident when skiing; it's something I know I'm good at. Dad has never mastered the art of snowboarding and was happily skiing the old-fashioned way with Ray and Martyn who are both of a similar level to him. I, however, love snowboarding and

116

can weave and wind down the mountain like a pro in comparison to them. I love speed and am not scared to aim for lumps and bumps on the piste at high speed to become airborne, where I can shimmy my board before landing.

"The polar bear dances!" Dad shouted.

They'd all been referring to me as the polar bear since I was not only stealing their thunder with my slick moves, but also with my posey white ski outfit. Kicking the slopes is the one time when I don't mind drawing attention to myself, and my new white salopettes and jacket did the job nicely. With go-faster black stripes across the chest of the jacket and knee pads, my outfit was suitably conspicuous amongst the prevailing array of skiers in their black ski pants and colourful jackets.

Dad wore a grey and blue combination with his bum bag a retro throwback to the eighties and his Nordica ski boots painfully archaic – he said he won't ever replace them since they're the first pair he has ever found to be comfortable. Martyn wore the obligatory black ski pants with a boring aubergine Puffa jacket, and Ray wore a red onesie that made him look like a ski-instructor from the eighties.

We stopped for lunch that day at our favourite restaurant at the summit of the three valleys resort, and there wasn't a single cloud in the sky. Skiers were crammed outside like sardines, lined up in deckchairs and huddled together on every available bench to enjoy the glorious sunshine, streaks of coloured sun lotion lining their faces. Placing our attire on the racks with the clutter of discarded sticks and skis, we ventured inside the wooden chalet, where we were shown to the last available table tucked in the corner.

Nothing out of the ordinary happened. Dad and his mates tried to be young and hip, and, as always, failed miserably. Ray encouraged me to have a shot of rum in my '*chocolat chaud*' which is the most decadent hot chocolate I have ever tasted; it is quite literally heaven in a cup, with its rich dark chocolate melted into hot milk, vanilla, and a generous dollop of thick cream on top. I agreed to the rum and told Dad to order me a portion of fries before removing my jacket and heading off to the toilet.

On my return the chocolat was already on the table, and the smirk on Ray's face made me nervous.

"What've you done?" I asked, as I sat at the table.

"What do you mean?" Dad said, a little too calmly.

"Have you put Ex-Lax in my hot chocolate?" I said, suspiciously.

"Don't be daft, I'm not *that* cruel." He looked at the others who failed to support his comment as they were remembering occasions when Dad had played his ridiculous jokes on them.

Ray is like an uncle to me, he and Lorraine have been fixtures in our home for most of my childhood, and if Mum and Dad ever went away together, I went to stay with them, feeling as much a part of their family unit as their own kids. I trusted him more than my own Dad at

118

times. But when Dad is around, he acts differently, as if Dad has put a kind of spell on him.

"Let's make haste while the sun shines," I said after I finished my chocolat and chips. The rum had a slightly exaggerated effect at such high altitude, and feeling a burst of euphoria, I was itching to get back to the enticing white playground outside and fill my lungs with its crisp alpine air.

Dad and Martyn burst into laughter. "You mean hay," Dad said.

God, I could have kicked myself. I'm always getting my sayings wrong, and Dad's the first to point out my faux pas when I make them.

"Make *hay* while the sun shines."

"Whatevs," I replied.

Once fully zipped up and ready for the cold embrace, we clambered across the crunchy snow in our cumbersome boots to reclaim our skis. I was relieved to find my new Burton Custom X board exactly where I'd left it.

My black boots strapped in place, we set off, Dad and the others whispering about something in their boyish huddle. No doubt they had spiked my hot chocolate thinking they'd see me make a spectacular nose-dive in the snow. But I would show them.

We had a great afternoon, the snow was perfect, and my board's sharp edges curved beautifully through the velvet snow, flexing, and popping in all the right places. There were no trees at the heights we were scaling, and

119

being the high season, the other skiers had carved out some amazing moguls which I loved jumping, while Dad and the others slalomed cautiously around each one.

The only thing that spoiled my exhilaration was standing in the lift queues. Not because of the time it took waiting for the lifts, but the unnerving sense that people were watching me, perhaps even talking about me. My French isn't good enough to translate, and each time I caught someone looking in my direction, my paranoia began to get the better of me.

"Dad, why do people keep staring at me, have I got chocolate on my face?" I asked.

"Don't be paranoid, son, nobody's looking at you." I couldn't see into his eyes, but the reflection in his mirrored sunglasses confirmed there was no chocolate moustache marking my upper lip.

On our last run down to the chalet we took the black run that was a heart-stopping precipice, testing all our nerves to the max.

"Don't shit yourself," Martyn said, as he set off in front of me. It crossed my mind again that they had snuck a laxative in my drink and were all waiting for its effects to take place, but my stomach felt fine. The effects of the rum were wearing off and my body, whilst exhausted, was tingling. No, I felt no different, but still had a sense that something was amiss.

Back at the chalet, we all slung our kit in the boot room and headed for the lounge. I hung my cropped jacket on the hook and was headed towards the sofa when Ray stopped me.

"Er, why don't you go and get changed before we have a drink and snack."

Before I could reply, Dad added, "Yes, perhaps go take a shower first." I looked at him confused. "I think that laxative may have taken effect."

I stood there knowing something was wrong, but still locked out of the joke that I suspected was on me. Heat began rising to my cheeks and I prayed that the burn from the mountain air disguised my blushing face. I headed off upstairs after warning them all that I would get my own back if they'd dared to do anything to me. But it was too late.

I checked in the vanity mirror and my face was glowing, white marks where my sunglasses had been, but nothing out of the ordinary. After having a quick shave, I turned on the shower before removing my salopettes and there it was…a huge dark brown smudge of chocolate all over the seat of my beautiful white salopettes. Some bastard had obviously put a puddle of chocolate on my chair at lunchtime and I hadn't noticed. In that split second, what I had thought to be my slightly inebriated paranoia became crystal clear. I had spent the afternoon out posing on the slopes with the entire ski population thinking I had soiled my pants.

I flew downstairs, my trousers in my hand, to be greeted by three young schoolboys sniggering; only Ray looked slightly ashamed of himself.

121

"It was your dad," Martyn said, trying to hold back his laughter.

"Oh, that's right, blame me!" Dad was laughing. I couldn't bring myself to say anything, showing any emotion right then would have been a result for Dad, whether funny or not, so I gave no reaction. I pushed the anger back down into its box and gave a raised eyebrow just like Mum as I turned and walked back to the shower that was waiting for me, silently screaming deep down inside.

My frustrated tears mixed with the shower water and I sobbed quietly as I scrubbed myself vigorously up and down until my skin was red raw. My mind replayed every moment that I had suspected someone looking at me in the lift queues – the painful, sympathetic looks of complete strangers who didn't have the heart to say anything, or the titters of laughter from those who fully bathed in the glory of Dad's practical joke.

Dad bought me a new pair of ski pants the next day, since despite an evening of scrubbing and soaking, a faint stain remained on my beautiful white salopettes. The new ones were black, which still went with my white jacket, but didn't compare to my silver-white ones that Mum had bought me the Christmas before. I didn't care; I no longer wanted to stand out on the slopes.

I lost all interest in skiing after the humiliation of that afternoon. Dad never apologised, and it was conveniently forgotten, just like all the other times. But I've never been skiing again since. I make my excuses, which are easier now that I'm with Rachel since she doesn't ski.

As a child I had so many expectations put on me. I know parents want us to learn right from wrong, appreciate all the things they give us, learn to be kind, and treat others as we wish to be treated ourselves… I'll pause on that one. Treat others as we wish to be treated? How would Dad have reacted if he had skied in front of his mates with a brown smear on his arse? How would he like to have a sign pinned to his back saying 'kick me', since that's how it felt with the thought of each person in the chairlift queue staring at my pristine white pants defiled with that shitty brown stain. It still fills me with horror to this day.

"No harm done," he'd said when he replaced my salopettes the following morning.

If he wasn't my dad, I would never have spoken to him again. I'd have treated him like I would treat the playground bully after leaving school, just given him an evil glare that said, 'I'll get you back, one day'. Instead, I disguised my emotions and took Dad's joke in my stride – I obeyed his silent rule with his mantra echoing in my mind,

'Be a good sport.'

Chapter 11

RONNIE

"How do I look?" Amanda asks, awkwardly fidgeting in front of the full-length mirror in our ensuite dressing room.

"Beautiful, hon," I reply. "A bit more lippy perhaps?"

She's wearing a designer dress I bought her last year. It's never seen the light of day up until now. I guess I was secretly trying to encourage her to wear a little more tasteful clothing when I bought it. Her wardrobe mainly consists of hacking jackets, thick bulky sweaters and jodhpurs. She lives in leggings at home, and I can't stand the things. It looks like she's wearing a pair of thick tights and they're not exactly sexy.

"The colour really suits you," I add.

The steel-blue strappy dress has a cowl neckline; the silk fabric hugs her moderately-sized breasts, and she's clearly not wearing a bra. She's all in proportion, and I had never realised I was bit of a 'breast' man until I met Penny. I try not to compare, but it's impossible not to get a flashback of those voluptuous firm tits bouncing around while she rides on top of me. I find myself imagining her in this same dress. There would be no creases around the bust line if she were to wear it, and probably a hint of her cleavage peeping out the top of the neckline.

"I love the necklace," Amanda says, straightening the tri-colour gold chain around her neck. I can tell that she does. It's subtle and she clearly feels comfortable wearing it, unlike the Rolex I bought her a few years ago. It remains locked in the safe in my office since she says she's worried about being mugged. I don't know why, being as she practically lives at the yard with her horses – hardly a target for daylight robbery.

I think it more likely that Amanda feels uncomfortable wearing any display of wealth; it's just not really her style. Amanda is more about experiences in life and enjoys holidays, nights out and so forth, but when it comes to indulgent gifts and spending, she always prefers to spend on others rather than herself. She didn't bat an eyelid at buying her mum a £500 Bosch dishwasher for Christmas, or treating her sister to a new laptop, and yet it took me years to persuade her we could comfortably afford a five grand holiday to the Caribbean…at least once a year.

I should be grateful really, if she were to be a social climber like my mother, or venture into the rat race with the likes of Meghan and other directors' wives, I could kiss goodbye to a hefty sum of money. The upkeep of youthful looks and having a designer outfit for every day of the year would certainly eat into my funds that I could be reinvesting in other businesses, so I'm secretly glad that Amanda has always held on to her roots.

She comes from a working-class background where money was sparse and her mother had to work two jobs to afford shoes and uniform for her and her sister. She was clearly taught from a young age to be cautious with what little money they had and if there's a way to save a few bob she's the first to find it. She still insists on buying vegetables from the market and meat from our local butcher where she barters to get a pound knocked off a bag of beef mince. I admire her prudence with money, but there are some things that annoy me. Her car for example; I don't know why she won't have a BMW or a nice Range Rover – plenty big enough for dogs or lugging a horse trailer around, and practical too. But no, she insists there is nothing wrong with her Vauxhall estate which is quite frankly embarrassing.

"Ronnie, please behave yourself tonight. No practical jokes! It's my birthday and I would like one day off from your antics in the year."

"Okay, sweetheart. I promise," I say half-heartedly. "I'll meet you in the hall. Don't be long, James will be here in ten."

I grab my lightweight Boss jacket before heading through to the bedroom. I'm on edge, and I don't want her to notice. If it doesn't all go to plan, I'll be devastated. It's been quite an undertaking getting everything arranged, and hopefully, if all goes well, there should be around forty to fifty guests waiting in the lounge when we get back from our meal.

Everyone is under strict instructions to arrive between six and six-thirty and turn off the lights in the lounge when I send a message to Martyn to say we're on our way home. Ray and Lorraine are meeting us for dinner, and only Ray and James are aware of what's happening. We're grabbing a meal in Prezzo's – not my idea. When Amanda learnt that we were heading off to see a show at Leatherhead Theatre which starts at seven-thirty, she insisted we go somewhere quick and simple to eat. She frequents Prezzo with her sister when she visits, and insists that they do the best Marinara pizza she's ever had. It's *her* birthday, so if it makes her happy…so be it. After the meal I'll pretend I've forgotten the tickets and come back home to fetch them and that will more than make up for the cheap meal. It will be such an unforgettable moment when the party is revealed.

I sit on the leather wing-backed chair in the entrance hall and grab my phone out of my pocket to check that everything is okay with Martyn and the pup. He should arrive first, and I'll give him the heads-up as soon as we're a safe distance away from the house.

I notice a message from Penny.

Hope it all goes to plan tonight. Thinking of you xx

I feel a stab of guilt. It's a double whammy. Not only do I feel bad that she is sat at home alone, having arranged tonight's proceedings, but somewhere deep down I also know it's wrong to be carrying on behind

Amanda's back. I know it can't go on indefinitely and I will find a way to cool things off with Penny one of these days. But like with most addictions, it's so hard to make that definite decision to stop. It's a case of *mañana*.

I go over everything in my head. Martyn has a key and knows the alarm code, his daughter Kiera has made one of her spectacular cakes – well two actually, since she's made a four and a zero which she's piped with blue icing – and I'm looking forward to seeing her masterpiece when we get back later. Caterers are bringing the food and drink at 6.45 p.m. precisely and will set everything out in the dining room. Amanda's stablehands, Belinda and Stacey, have sorted out helium balloons and have instructions where the other decorations are hidden which they're going to arrange in the lounge. Penny has arranged two waitresses to arrive with the caterers and they will also be on cloakroom duty, ensuring everyone's coats and jackets are out of sight before serving canapés and champagne after we arrive.

My phone interrupts my reverie.

Outside Dad – bang on time, as always.

I call to Amanda as I hear the gravel crunching outside. She arrives with freshly-applied lippie in a deep plum colour that I approve of, and a black velvet jacket that I feel somehow spoils the elegance of her dress. A pashmina or bolero style jacket would have suited it better.

"Have you got the tickets?" she asks, heading for the front door.

"Yes," I lie, tapping my jacket pocket. I enter the code on our alarm system, checking that the kitchen/breakfast room is omitted for Daisy to have free run of the area.

Chapter 12

JAMES

"What are we going to see at the theatre?" Rachel asks.

I hate lying to her, but according to Dad there's some Simon and Garfunkel show running, which he thinks Mum will be fooled by.

"Simon and Garfunkel," I say, zipping up her black velvet dress and kissing her neck.

"Who're they?"

I look at her reflection in the mirror. She is stunning as always, her black velvet dress hugging her curves and her décolletage notably impressive.

"You're kidding, right?"

"No."

"A folk-rock duo from the sixties and seventies. They sang 'Scarborough Fair'." Rachel looks at me blankly in the mirror. I start humming the tune to her as I help her on with her jacket, taking in the divine smell of her Chanel perfume.

"Oh yeah," she says unconvincingly.

Despite playing the guitar, I have a lousy voice. Something that I discovered when getting past the beginner stages of learning the guitar, since the two go together. Dad would say *There's not much point in playing pop songs if you can't sing them,* but it gave me something to do when I was a kid, and when Mum bought me my first electric guitar, I learnt the first few bars of 'Smoke on the Water,' picturing myself playing in a band one day.

Robert was the only person who thought I was great on the guitar; he would try and strum along with my acoustic guitar but could never manage the F chord and his fingers were too stubby to hold a barre chord. He could sing though; I was always envious of his ease in singing along to almost any tune. Both my guitars sit at the back of a cupboard gathering dust now.

After we left college, Robert went to Leeds University to study criminal law (something my parents relished with exaggerated congratulations as if to highlight my failure) and we only seem to catch up on special occasions these days, like our twenty-firsts, or Robert's graduation celebration – and Mum's fortieth birthday. It's another reason I feel a little nervous about tonight. He's coming along to Mum's party, and I haven't been able to tell Rachel.

Rachel and I head downstairs.

"I'll just feed Bella," she says, strolling towards the kitchen, but I stop her.

"I've already done it. And she's got plenty of water," I say. I fed her double the usual amount and don't want Rachel to see this since we're staying over at Mum and

Dad's tonight, and I've already packed a bag and hidden it in the boot of the car.

"I'll just grab your mum's present, you grab the keys," Rachel says.

We've bought Mum a bronze ornament of an Arabian horse. We couldn't stretch to a Lladro, but the curves on this piece are beautiful and I know she'll think it looks just like Starlight.

Rachel appears with the beautifully-wrapped gift, in a striking dark floral box with red ribbon tied in a perfect bow on top – she's a stickler for detail. I'm not sure which looks more beautiful, the elegant gift or my gorgeous fiancée. I squeeze the end of her cute button nose, noticing the familiar freckles that melt my heart and her hair which is swept up displaying elegant sparkly diamante earrings. I think she looks like a princess. My princess.

"Have I told you lately?"

"I love you too, James," she says, giving me a kiss that lingers for just long enough that I question whether we have time to go back to the bedroom and carefully undress again.

"We'll be late." She knows my every thought. Even the naughty ones. Despite the fact that we've only being together eighteen months, I sometimes think she knows me better than I know myself. She's sensed my anxiety a few times today, and I've told her I'm just nervous because it's Mum's birthday and I don't want Dad getting up to any stupid pranks. Which is partly true.

"She knows how to handle him, James. Stop worrying, it'll be fine."

But then she knows me too well. I do worry. My nightmares are still troubling me, despite having a couple of sessions with my counsellor, Lucas.

The inevitable happened in my last appointment, and Lucas began to probe about my childhood, which I find so tedious. I don't really remember my early years, and I told him there are far more happy memories than bad. We talked about the holidays I went on as a young child and how I enjoyed them, especially when I made friends in hotels we stayed at, giving me the momentary joy of a pretend brother or sister to play with.

But talking through my upbringing doesn't seem to have made any difference to my nightmares – not yet anyway. I don't see what difference talking about past memories will make, especially with regards my work situation. I want to focus on the new memories that Rachel and I will make, including travelling.

We both love travelling abroad, but for the foreseeable future that will have to be put on hold since we need to spend every last penny on renovations in our new home. We certainly won't be holidaying at Ray and Lorraine's place in Malaga again, not after the stunt Dad pulled last year.

Mum and Dad kindly offered to pay for us to go with them, and Mum and Rachel got to know each other better, which was lovely. They're already like mother and daughter, and I think she fills a void for Mum just as much as she does for me. But Dad went and spoilt things, as usual, when he played his oh-so-glorious prank on me and Rachel that nearly gave me a heart attack. When I think about it, that was possibly when the migraines started again.

Chapter 13

RONNIE

The restaurant is quiet, being it's so early. We have three double tables pushed together set for six. James is wearing a white T-shirt under a black jacket and despite wearing jeans, looks fairly smart in a rock star kind of way. He holds the chair for Rachel as she takes her place in the centre next to him, with a spare seat waiting for Ray. I sit opposite her with Amanda beside me, waiting for Lorraine.

I check my phone and assume that no news is good news. My message has been sent to Martyn, so I assume everything is underway at home, and I feel a bubble of excitement imagining everyone en route. The anticipation of seeing Amanda's face when she discovers what I've pulled off feels like the best prank I've ever played. She's going to be blown away when she sees her horsey buddies, friends and family all waiting at home, and I'm expecting tears when she meets the new puppy.

As I place the napkin on my lap, I note how it's made of heavyweight paper; not quite your cheap paper napkin but missing the luxury of cotton or linen. I look over my shoulder through the front window. It's still light outside, but there's no sign of Ray and Lorraine. *Where the hell are they?* Ray knows how het up I am about tonight, and I told him to meet us here at six.

"Would you like to order some drinks?" The waitress stands at our table, a young blonde girl dressed in a short black skirt and tight black T-shirt with a little grey apron tied around her minute waist.

"I think we'll wait for our friends to arrive – "

"No," I interrupt James. "Let's order some fizz, and they can order their drinks when they get here." I need to relax; I can hear the tension in my own voice.

"I'll just have a mineral water with lime please," Rachel says. It seems strange she's not drinking, since James is driving.

"A Bud Light for me," James says.

"And a bottle of champagne please," I add.

The waitress looks uncomfortable.

"We only have prosecco, I'm afraid, sir."

"Then your finest bottle of prosecco, please," I say, "and some bread and olives for the table." We won't have time for starters, I decide. Not if I'm to convince Amanda that we have time to rush home and get the tickets.

A distraction is required. I may have a little fun with the waitress tonight, I decide, being she's so young.

Ray and Lorraine arrive and give their jackets to the waitress by the door before rushing over to greet us.

"Sorry we're late," Lorraine says, pecking me on the cheek.

"Couldn't find anywhere to park," Ray adds.

"Happy birthday, darling." Lorraine hands a beautifully gift-wrapped parcel to Amanda, who jumps up to kiss her and give her a warm embrace.

After seating themselves at the table, Amanda carefully opens the gift, to reveal a beautiful silver bangle with a clasp shaped into a horse's bridle to hold it together.

"I love it. What a thoughtful gift," Amanda says.

"I suggested a leather horsewhip," Ray says, "but thought Ronnie may be a little old to start getting into BDSM."

Once the surge of laughter dissipates, I announce one of my ritual games that I know will annoy Amanda, but she'll go along with it – she's a good sport. "You get the first forfeit tonight, for being late." I smile at Ray.

"Count me out," Amanda says matter-of-factly.

"And me," Rachel says. She seems a little off this evening. I can't quite put my finger on it, but there's a sombre air about her. Usually she's great fun, and bursting with conversation, but she's subdued and notably pale. Hopefully, she'll liven up at the party later.

"So, when the waitress comes over, you have to ask her for a St Clements."

Ray groans. He's been a victim of this request before, but the old ones are always the best. Judging by the age of our waitress, she won't have a clue what a St Clements is, and it will throw her into a frenzy.

"What's the prize?" Ray asks, eager to know what I'll have to sacrifice.

"The satisfaction of me footing the bill tonight," I reply.

"You're on!"

The waitress meanders over to take our food orders, and Ray interrupts, explaining that he and Lorraine haven't ordered any drinks yet.

"Of course, sir, what would you like?" she replies obligingly.

"A gin and slimline tonic for my wife, please. And I'll have a St Clements." He has a perfectly straight face, as he waits for the response. The waitress hesitates, not knowing whether to admit that she has no idea what he has just asked for or not. I love the awkward moment, exacerbated by the fact that Ray doesn't put her out of her misery. To my disappointment, Amanda jumps in.

"It's orange juice with bitter lemon," she says,

"Of course," the waitress replies, smiling. "I'll be back with the drinks and to take your orders in a bit." And she sweeps away back towards the bar.

After the usual indecision from Amanda and Lorraine, we're all finally ready to place our orders, and the waitress returns. We all stare in wonder as she places a glass of orange juice in front of Ray. It's clearly not a St Clements, as there is no sign of any fizz in the glass, just a small piece of lemon bobbing in the middle like a rubber duck in a swimming pool.

"You've got a 'bit' of lemon there, Ray," I say, a snigger escaping as I try to suppress the full blast of laughter that wants to escape.

"That's right, isn't it?" the waitress says, looking at Amanda. "You said a bit of lemon with orange juice?"

James lets out a snigger, which sets me off; he doesn't tend to laugh at my jokes these days – probably thinks he's too grown up now he's nearly a married man.

Amanda intervenes, killing my laughter. "No, sorry, love, we meant *bitter lemon*. It's a fizzy sour lemon drink, Schweppes usually make it."

The waitress blushes and takes the drink away while Ray and I collapse in a heap, tears pouring down our faces. It's the first time we've seen the drink interpreted in this way.

"Ssh, Ronnie, are we going to eat tonight, or what?" Amanda says.

She's got a point. I check my watch and it's nearly quarter past six. We need to get a move on if I'm to convince her about the tickets for the show.

"You should see what James and Rachel bought me for my birthday," Amanda says, going to great lengths to describe the large lump of metal that I'm to have displayed at home with Amanda's other hideous knick-knacks.

The waitress returns, flustered. "I'm sorry, sir, we don't have any bitter lemon, I can do you an orange juice with lemonade?" she says.

"Don't worry, please. I'll just have some of the wine," Ray replies, grabbing the bottle of prosecco from the table to pour himself a glass.

"Can I take your orders, please?" With her notebook to the ready, we all take it in turns to order our main meals. I order myself a pepperoni pizza, since I'm not overly keen on pasta dishes apart from spaghetti Bolognese, which I only like the way Amanda makes it.

"Can you please make sure it has no garlic on it," I say. The waitress nods her head. She still seems embarrassed by the whole drink thing, which we've all forgotten already. "And would you mind telling the chef that we're in a bit of a rush – we have a show to see at seven-thirty," I add.

The first few plates of food arrive fifteen minutes later, and as the waitress returns to the kitchen to fetch Ronnie and James's meals, Ray decides it's payback time,

"Plate swipe," he says.

I should have known.

To get me back, he's asked me to put my plate on my lap and pretend the waitress never brought it to the table. It never fails to stop the waiting staff in their tracks. "What's it worth?" I say.

"Honestly, you're like a couple of schoolchildren," Amanda scolds us, putting her napkin on her lap and giving me one of her glares. Ray ignores her admonition.

"A bottle of Bollinger," he says.

"They don't sell it here." I laugh as I take a sip from my glass.

"Then I'll gift you one from my cellar," he adds, not to be defeated.

To be honest, I would have done the dare without any reward. It's easy for me to carry this one out, and I swiftly grab my plate and hold it under the table on my lap just as the waitress returns with the final meals.

"Okay, is that everything?" she asks.

"Er, no, I think there's a pepperoni pizza to come."

Her cheeks flush as she stares at the empty space where my plate was, my vacant expression throwing her into a spin. "Oh," she stutters, with her eyebrows furrowed. "I thought... I'll be right back." She scoots off towards the kitchen again. Ray and I burst out laughing, and I glance at James for approval, but he seems a little po-faced.

I put the plate back on the table and we all start to tuck in to our food just as the waitress returns looking somewhat distressed. "I'm sorry, sir, but..." She pauses when she sees my plate is back on the table. She shakes her head in confusion.

"It's okay," I say. "We were just playing a little game with you."

She gives a nervous giggle as she turns to leave. I call her back. "Er, excuse me, could we please have another bottle of prosecco?"

"Certainly," she says, eager to get back to her serving station.

"Poor girl, you'd better leave her a good tip," Rachel says, a wry smile edging the corners of her mouth. She's used to me and my pranks, and I know she usually quite enjoys my sense of humour, although since the whole cat thing, and the shock of thinking I'd dropped poor Bella over the balcony, I sense she's not quite so amused by me anymore.

It's ten to seven, and after suggesting that we treat ourselves to ice-creams at the theatre to save time with desserts, Lorraine says, "Good idea, gets me out of forfeits."

"Oh no," I reply. "When the waitress comes to ask if we want any dessert, you need to ask for something before we ask for the bill."

"What?" she asks, with one eyebrow slightly raised.

"A St Clements."

"What? We've already played that one, Ronnie."

"I know, which is why it's so funny, the stakes rise. You've got to act as if none of it happened earlier and be completely innocent. You've got to be convincing though."

The table falls silent, and everyone looks at me in disbelief – it's brilliant!

"What's the reward?" Lorraine asks, a reluctant tone in her voice. "It'd better be good."

"You get to drive my car tomorrow when we go to quiz night." She stares at me, not quite believing that I would let her loose in my pride and joy. "Ray can drive by and pick Amanda up, and you and I will go in the Aston."

Ray looks at me, confused. He knows that I don't like other people handling my beast, but it's only a five-to-ten-minute drive to the local pub where we go for the Sunday night quiz. We went along to join James and Rachel a few months back, and loved it so much, we decided to bring Ronnie and Lorraine along to make up a team. We call ourselves the 'A-Team'.

James is biting his nails again, probably as nervous as I am at the thought of Lorraine driving my car.

"You're on," Lorraine says.

"Can I get you anything else?" the waitress asks.

I make as if to speak, but Lorraine interrupts me. "Could I have another drink please?" She says this whilst staring directly at the waitress. *Great eye contact.*

"Of course, another gin and tonic?" The waitress seems self-satisfied that she remembers what Lorraine is drinking.

"Actually, could I have a St Clements please?" Lorraine says.

The waitress's face is a picture. Confusion at first, breaking out into a nervous smile. I can almost feel her heart racing. Amanda is looking away, cringing with embarrassment. James and Ronnie are sporting their best poker faces, as am I.

"It's orange juice with bitter lemon," Lorraine adds. I'm amazed by her spectacular performance. Her

143

innocence is worthy of an Oscar, and there's no hint of a smile on her face.

I tilt my face away from the waitress. I can't look; I'm going to lose it any minute.

"Oh, and the bill please," Ray says.

"Of course, sir. I'll be right back." The bewildered waitress heads off towards the kitchen and we all burst into fits of laughter.

"Okay, you win tonight, Lorraine," I say. "That was a sterling performance."

I look at my watch; we need to get a move on if my story is to be feasible. It's a ten-minute drive home and then a fifteen-minute drive back to the theatre. The nerves are kicking in again; everyone should be in place by now. If anyone or anything screws this up before we enter the lounge, I'll be beside myself with rage.

The waitress returns with the bill and is about to say something.

"It's okay," I say, "we were joking about the St Clements. I'm sorry, we were just having a bit of fun." I find myself feeling slightly sorry for her now.

"Oh, I see," she says, smiling.

Bless her, she's probably only about eighteen, and we've really put her through her paces tonight. I'll leave a thirty-pound tip, although these days, the tips all get shared amongst the staff – which I don't agree with.

The restaurant has filled up a little as we all make to leave. There are early signs of the golden hour forming outside; the sky is melting into pastel shades and there's a sense of stillness in the air. We part company from Lorraine and Ray.

"See you at the theatre," Amanda says, kissing Lorraine.

As we approach James's car, I start to pat and pretend to search each of my inside pockets, feigning concern.

"What's wrong?" Amanda asks.

"Shit, I thought I had the tickets in my jacket pocket," I say,

"Come on, Ronnie, you're not funny."

"No, I'm being deadly serious. James, you'll have to drive us home quickly so I can pick them up."

"Oh for Christ's sake, Ronnie," Amanda says, getting into the back of James's car.

Rachel raises her eyebrows at James as if she's running out of patience too. It confirms that James has kept my secret and not told her about the surprise party – he's always so reliable.

"You'd better put your foot down," Rachel says, as she plugs her seatbelt in. "It's only twenty-five minutes until the show starts."

Amanda barely looks at me as we pull away, obviously annoyed at my lack of organisation. She's in for a hell of a shock. We haven't had a party at ours since my fortieth nearly six years ago. She's going to love it, and I can't wait to pull off the biggest surprise of her lifetime.

Chapter 14

JAMES

We're en route to pick up Mum and Dad for dinner, when Rachel lets it slip that she knows about the surprise party. It triggers massive insecurity, and the familiar bilious feeling stirs in my stomach.

"Why didn't you tell me, Rach?"

"Why didn't *you* tell me?"

"Because Dad told me not to."

"Which is *why* I was playing along with it," she says impatiently.

"Well, I can't believe you haven't told me. I feel stupid now, and Dad will be furious if he thinks I told you."

"Oh, for God's sake, James, I'm just as good at acting surprised as you are, he's not going to know and besides, stop being so scared of your father. You're a grown adult now, you don't need to be nervous of him."

That's easy for her to say. There's a fine line between respect and fear. You grow up learning everything you know in life because of your parents, and there isn't a time or date when you suddenly say *Okay, I'm all grown up now so stop laying down the rules – I can do this on my own.* No. We're obliged to show our respect by continuing by their rules both spoken and unspoken for fear of repercussion or disapproval.

I don't want to discuss my feelings with Rachel, but I feel so triggered. How long has she kept it from me that she's known about tonight? Why does she have to reprimand me about fearing Dad? It's not true. She doesn't understand.

Last week, Lucas asked me to recall a time when I felt I had disappointed Dad, and the one that sprang to mind was the time he took me along to a poker match to teach me the basics. It was the time I felt that insidious feeling of shame most clearly.

We went to some club where he plays snooker and a small group of us stayed behind to play poker. One of the bar staff was paid to act as croupier and I remember thinking it all seemed a bit serious for a card game. Chairs were brought in and set up around one of the snooker tables, and all the lights were turned off apart from the strip light over our table. Drinks were set up on the bar along with poker chips for the game and ashtrays placed on the snooker table that had a red cloth thrown across it.

Jeremy was there, who I'd only met once before, and apart from Bob from the office, I didn't know anyone else around the table. I felt a knot in my stomach as I looked around the table at the strangers' faces, like I was in a scene from some gangster movie. The barmaid smiled at me, sensing my apprehension, and I smiled back, shrinking further into my seat.

Once the game began, I was fascinated – not so much with the rules of the game, which I knew a little about anyway, but rather with watching Dad. I had never seen him so serious; his face never once changed expression other than the odd raise of his eyebrows, which seemed to follow no pattern. I watched as he became this calm and collected person that I hardly recognised; every movement from placing his cigarette in the ashtray to picking up his cards seemed precise and poised, but I could feel the competitiveness oozing from his every pore. He seemed oblivious to the fact I was there sitting next to him, and when I nudged him, he disregarded me with a flick of his hand like I was a fly or something.

My nerves increased. He had far too much money on the table and the thought of him losing five grand was making me feel queasy. I wanted him to stop.

"Dad," I tried to whisper in his ear.

"Shh." I flinched at his reaction. "Do you have a bet you want to place on the table?" His tone was cold and clinical. I didn't have any chips of course, and everyone looked at me as I cringed with embarrassment, wishing I hadn't interrupted. I lowered my head as I felt my cheeks burn.

Well, Dad lost his five thousand pounds that night, and at eighteen, it seemed like a crazy amount of money to me. So much so that I mentioned it to Mum the next time I saw her, and I knew by the look on her face that I'd made a mistake. Her wide eyes told me she was just as shocked as I was at how much he'd lost, and the creases on her forehead and her tight-lipped expression showed how angry she was. It caused a row between them, with Mum making him promise to pack in his game nights. I wasn't to find this out until later.

Dad picked me up from the station some three weeks later, and I'd forgotten all about the poker night. I jumped into the front passenger seat to be greeted with an icy cold stare.

"Hi, Pops." I was excited to tell him about my night out at a gig, but I was greeted with a stony silence.

"Next time you want to play with the big boys, don't go crying to your mother."

"Huh?"

"I'm banned from poker because of you; you really ought to learn when to keep your mouth shut." Then he turned the radio on.

I was horrified, and I can't say reliving the experience with my counsellor did anything to ease the soul-destroying angst of disappointing my dad. It brought back the feeling of wanting to run to my room like a little boy and hug Max, crying into his fur and letting him lick the tears from my face. That in turn, led me to explaining how we lost Max recently and how I miss him more than anyone or anything I've ever lost before. Tears streamed down my face as I explained that it felt worse than losing both my grandfathers, but Lucas consoled me, explaining

149

how we miss our loved ones according to how big a part they play in our daily life. Max was there for me every day from ten years old until I left home at nineteen, and Lucas seemed to understand that Max was so much more than just a pet to me.

We pull up outside Mum and Dad's house.

"But how did you find out about the party?" I say to Rachel.

"Shh, not now."

Mum waves as she approaches the car, looking stunning in a blue silk dress, and she looks so happy. I feel a knot of nerves and excitement at the thought of the surprise that will be waiting for her when we return later. My conversation with Rachel will have to wait.

The café is quiet and I sit down in front of Mum, with Rachel to my side; Dad always insists on alternate boy-girl seating in his old-fashioned way.

"Are you okay, sweetheart?" Dad says as Rachel puts her hand across the top of her glass to stop him filling it with prosecco. I'm worried about her headache too, it's not like her, but it's probably just hormonal changes or something. Still, I'm touched that Dad shows his concern.

The meal is unbearably stressful with Dad playing his usual pranks and winding up the waitress. I'm about to tell him to pack it in, when Mum catches my eye, giving me that acknowledging look she always does, which expresses the need to pacify him and let him have his fun. I try not to cringe as I sit and watch how he humiliates the poor young girl serving us and fix a smile on my face when Dad looks my way, to show nothing but pure amusement when inside I feel sick. Sick to the pit of my stomach knowing what that uncertainty and torrent of confusion feels like. How her heart rate is pounding waiting for the moment where someone will step in and rescue her, take the blame for whatever or whoever is the invisible antagonist threatening her sense of wellbeing. She probably thinks she's going mad.

I must admit I feel some relief when I watch someone else being the butt of Dad's gags – so long as I'm watching him winding someone else up, I know I'm safe. He laughs and takes credit for his results as if he's the greatest showman on earth, but my acting is just as accomplished as his, when it needs to be.

It feels an age before my cannelloni eventually arrives, but my appetite has waned. Rachel makes to take a piece of the steaming hot pasta from my dish, but I shoo her fork away with my hand. I don't do sharing, not with food. Another anxiety of mine is sharing from others' glass or plate. It's not that I fear Rachel will contaminate me with her germs as such, but there's a privacy that surrounds one's food and drink. It makes me feel physically sick to touch food that isn't my own, and likewise, people need to respect they can't touch mine either.

"Sorry, I forgot," she says, giving me an apologetic look.

My head is buzzing, as if a migraine is threatening. There's a strange sense of feeling I'm outside of my own body and I'm looking in on everyone. It reminds of being high, only I haven't had a spliff since I started dating Rachel. I look at the prosecco in the ornate silver bucket and ponder how I feel like this without having touched it. Perhaps I should switch to fizzy water instead of my beer, since I need a clear head to drive home after the meal.

As Rachel puts her hand on my knee and leans in to peck me on the check, I'm aware that something feels different tonight. It is as though she and I are the only responsible adults whilst Dad, Ray, and Lorraine are like children as they carry on with Dad's forfeits. He could offer me a five-star honeymoon in the Maldives, and I still wouldn't entertain him by joining in. I'm done with pandering to his ego and humiliating other people.

I glare at Lorraine when she's lured to prank the waitress with an offer of driving Dad's car. I don't know which annoys me more, the fact Dad would let her drive his car, or the fact they all gatecrash what was my and Rachel's night out at the pub quiz. Typical of Dad, he insisted on coming along one week, and got all competitive. We won that week, which of course he thought was entirely because of him, so that was it. He wanted to come again and then started to invite their friends along. I don't mean to sound selfish, and I know Rachel enjoys having Mum there, but sometimes it feels like I don't get any space. I work for the company, we live only ten minutes down the road from home, we're summoned to visit at least once a week, Dad pops round to see how the house is coming along, and now they come to our quiet night out on a Sunday evening. It's suffocating.

I look at Dad, who is confidently holding court.

"Are you alright, James?" Mum's noticed.

"Yeah, I think I'll just go outside and get some fresh air."

I remove myself from the table to go outside and light a cigarette. As I inhale, my head spins a little and I feel a buzzing in my ears. Everyone I love is sitting inside, my family, friends and beautiful fiancée. So why do I feel so agitated? Why do I have a sense of feeling unsafe?

It's not even dark yet, which is one of my worst phobias. I can't be alone in the dark; I don't even like driving at night alone, which is something I struggle to hide at times. Rachel understands though, she's so caring and gentle, and I trust her. She makes no fuss about me having a bedside light on during the night, even though she doesn't understand fully why I'm afraid. I didn't either, until Lucas dragged it out of me.

Chapter 15

RONNIE

As the car crunches onto the driveway, the house ahead is dark. I texted Martyn en route to say we were on our way, and hopefully, they're all poised in the lounge waiting to turn the lights on and hit the 'play' button for Stevie Wonder's 'Happy Birthday'.

Shit! The front door's ajar. Who the heck forgot to close the front door? Before I have a chance to act, Amanda notices,

"Why's the front door open?"

"I don't know, you were last out?" I say.

"The alarm isn't going off? I know I shut it, Ron." She sounds nervous.

"You wait here, I'll go and check it out," I say, thinking on my feet. I'll kill the stupid bugger that didn't close it.

James edges the car up to the front door and turns off the engine. I jump out and cautiously peer around the edge of the door before creeping slowly through to the hallway to make it seem that I'm nervous. I open the cloaks cupboard and see the alarm is disarmed – as it should be. Someone clearly forgot to shut the front door.

The house is eerily quiet; no evidence of any life. I have an awful feeling for a moment that perhaps nobody has arrived. I look at the heavy double oak doors to the lounge and pray that there is a room of people on the other side. I return to the car.

"It's all okay," I say, "but perhaps we should give the whole place a quick once-over. I can't remember where I left the tickets, anyway."

Amanda reluctantly gets out of the car, edging her way to the front door with James and Rachel in pursuit.

"Sweetheart, it's fine. Daisy would be barking if anything was wrong." I encourage Amanda in through the front door and put my arm around her, steering her towards the double doors of our lounge. I prepare to open them.

"I think I left the tickets on the table in here," I say, barely concealing the excitement in my voice.

I open the doors and the moment I pull her through, the lights turn on and she jumps with fright as party poppers spray in all directions.

"Surprise!" The chorus of our guests' voices is joined by Stevie Wonder. Amanda puts her hand to her mouth, her shock slowly fading as she takes in the scene.

The generously-sized lounge is full of people dressed up in their finest – black sparkly dresses and low-cut jumpsuits on the women, chinos and smart shirts on the men. One or two have gone over the top, like Meghan, who is wearing a black and gold Gatsby-style dress, and Lorraine's hairdresser Monique, who is dressed in some nude sequin number that looks like she's naked at first glance. Blue and silver balloons are hanging from the corners of the room, and a large number 40 hangs from the mantelpiece. There is an archway of glitter balloons over the patio doors and the bar is laden with beautifully-wrapped gifts decorated with large bows and curled ribbon.

Amanda is clearly overwhelmed, rendered speechless as people start to approach and greet her. She looks at me...

"But what about—"

"The show?" I say, grinning. "A decoy."

She's about to hug me, when she clocks her cousin from up north who she hasn't seen for nearly a year. "Oh my God, Karen!" They hug and kiss, while James and Rachel come and pat me on the back.

"Well done, Pops," James says, grinning.

"What, you knew about this?" Rachel says, clearly stunned.

"Are we late for the party?" The voices come from the hallway, and Ray and Lorraine join us, looking nearly as smug as I do when they're greeted with the spectacle. They head over towards their daughter Kiera, whom I'm glad to see is wearing a dress that covers her thighs for once.

I work my way around all our guests, thanking them for coming and making sure that Tillie and Freya, our waitresses for the evening, keep everyone's glasses topped up. I spend a little longer with Emma, Amanda's sister. She seems a little uncomfortable mingling amongst our friends, many of whom she's never met.

"Thank you so much for doing this for Amanda, such a lovely surprise," she says, pecking me on the cheek. We make polite conversation, until I find my excuse to finally pull away.

"The best surprise is yet to come," I say as my eyes search the room for Martyn.

As I watch everyone chatting and nibbling on canapés, Martyn finds me first. He taps me on the shoulder. "Should we bring in the pièce de resistance?"

"Where is he?" I ask, glancing in the direction of Amanda to ensure we're not overheard.

"We left him in the garage so he wouldn't have to spend too much time shoved in a box. Do you want me to get him?"

"No, you're fine, mate, I'll fetch him. Thanks."

Amanda's face is a picture when I beckon her over to the oversized box which I place on the lounge carpet. James lowers the music a little, and everyone stands watching with bated breath as she strokes the top of the box and slowly removes the gigantic blue bow. Martyn has his camcorder poised, filming the whole thing.

"Here we go again, how many boxes are inside this one?" Amanda laughs, confident that I've carried out my usual joke where I wrap layer upon layer with a tiny little gift box in the centre in which will be some item of jewellery. I encourage her to start lifting the lid before the puppy lets out a whimper or scratches at the box from the inside.

"Oh, Ronnie!" She squeals with delight with the sight of the bedazzled pup looking up at her with its big brown eyes and huge ears that flop forwards. As she reaches in, the puppy jumps straight into her arms, licking her face and biting her hands the way puppies do. The room erupts with oohs and aahs and Rachel and Lorraine are first to rush and greet the new puppy. I can feel my grin spreading across my face, and the sting of a few tears that well up with happiness.

I've done it!

My wife has had a fortieth birthday that she'll never forget.

Chapter 16

JAMES

The party turns out to be one of Dad's better ideas. Mum deserves all the attention she gets on her big birthday. She's always been the underdog, meekly going along with whatever Dad's plans are, whilst ensuring he's treated like a king in his home. She's such a good wife; the house is spotless, there's always homemade food on the table, and she carries out all the chores that Dad doesn't show any interest in. It's hardly a modern-day set-up, and I intend to support Rachel in our new home a lot more than Dad does with Mum.

It's great to watch Mum mingling with all her friends and family. Well, not much family really, since neither of my grandmothers could make it, which is the excuse Dad made for not inviting Rachel's parents. He said if grandparents couldn't attend, it didn't seem fair to invite the in-laws, but I know it's because he finds them slightly stuffy. Rachel hasn't said anything though, so it would seem she doesn't mind.

The house has the perfect lounge for a party, probably the floor space of the entire downstairs of our little house. It has a grand entrance with double oak doors that lead to two steps down into the bar area. The mahogany bar, Dad's pride and joy, is like a mini pub with three back mirrors and shelves for all his drinks. It has six leather stools, each of which is occupied, beside a large floor space where people can dance later once they've loosened up.

The birthday decorations don't really blend with the colour scheme. I never understood why my parents insisted on an aubergine corner suite, but it's soft and bouncy and is great for spreading out on when watching the superscreen TV. The windows are all draped with elaborate curtains, which are so old-fashioned – blinds would look much better, but thankfully balloons are covering most of them tonight.

This house always feels like an elaborately decorated gift box to me, which is empty inside once you peel off all the layers of wrapping. As a child, Mum and Dad never used to kiss or touch the way Ray and Lorraine did; there wasn't the warmth and sense of connection that I witnessed in their home. Just an emptiness which, when I look back now, I can interpret. They were (and still are) like brother and sister that happened to have a child – me, who somehow glued them together. I often wonder if Mum hadn't accidentally fallen pregnant with me, whether they would have married at all.

As I watch them this evening, things haven't changed – Mum's happy chatting to Aunty Emma, Meghan, and her old schoolfriends, while Dad laughs with Martyn, Ray and Cousin George, drinking red wine and chain-smoking. He's such a blokey bloke, the sort that goes into the other room for a cigar with the men after a get-together while the women are left to natter and do the tidying up.

I've often wondered if either Mum or Dad has had, or is having an affair. But Mum is hardly the type. She's more interested in her horses, and other than occasional nights out with Lorraine or Meghan, she never makes much effort with her appearance, which I'm sure she would do if there were a new man in her life. Dad is hardly the type either, always obsessing with his next big tennis tournament or business venture, and he would never risk upsetting Mum, or me come to think of it. No, I think they've just grown into a dull middle-aged couple, complacent with their relationship, and Dad finding his extramarital fun by thinking up his next way to prank someone. If there's one ambition I have in life, it's to ensure that Rachel and I never become like them; I want us to remain friends *and* lovers into old age, and I will always put her first, above everything else in life.

Judging by Rachel's face, she was totally unaware that Dad was buying Mum a new German Shepherd. Mum has tears in her eyes as she greets the cute bundle of fluff and it reminds me of the day we got Max. It has huge-oversized paws waiting to be grown into, a honeyed ruff around its neck which contrasts against the black and brown smudges on its face, and the most adorable ears that fold over like bookmarks. Strangely, I don't gush with delight like the rest of the room; it would feel disloyal to Max. He's not been gone a year and it seems Mum and Dad have already found a replacement for him.

Rachel is fussing over Daisy, whose entire rear end is swaying as she wags her tail, when Robert arrives. He's always late. I take in how great he looks, almost hipster in his skinny jeans and black and red checked shirt. His scruffy beard makes him look older than his twenty-four years and he's just landed himself a job training with some private law firm. It's the first time he's met Rachel, and I'm beaming with pride as she charms him with her contagious confidence.

"So, how did you keep such a stunning girl a secret from me?" Robert asks.

Rachel chuckles at the compliment. "Well, you must know what this family is like for keeping secrets," she says.

And she's right. I'm just as good at keeping quiet about surprises as Dad is. I feel a huge sense of satisfaction that at last I have a secret that Dad doesn't know about. For the first time in my life, I have a piece of information that will shock him to his senses. I've been itching to tell Mum, but I know I can't. It wouldn't be fair, and I want to see her full reaction when she finds out. When the time is right, I know I'm going to feel the proudest I've ever felt in my entire life.

Chapter 17

RONNIE

There was only one minor puppy accident throughout the evening, and since Amanda was enjoying herself socialising, I thought it only fair that I clean up the little puddle. I mopped it up with some kitchen roll and then sprayed some anti-bac cleaner on the carpet. No doubt I'll get told off tomorrow for doing it wrong, but it's not usually my job to deal with dog dilemmas or house cleaning matters.

The party was a roaring success, and everyone congratulated me on pulling it off. Champagne was flowing, the canapés were to die for (especially the little arancini balls which had been warmed in the oven) and Amanda even got me up dancing to Michael Jackson. The waitresses did a fantastic job, even washing all the glasses up after people had left. I paid them each a healthy tip for all their hard work and they finally left around midnight after explaining that the company would be back on Monday to pick up any last bits and pieces.

It's down to a select few now. Ray, James, Martyn and I are on the port, while our wives giggle away on more bubbly. Rachel had a headache, bless her (I knew something wasn't quite right) so she's gone off to bed. Amanda settled her in to her favourite guest room with the pink Laura Ashley print.

Martyn and Meghan are all-nighters, so no doubt I'll have to kick them out in an hour or so. Ray and Lorraine are staying over and will take one of the other guest rooms; Ray secretly packed an overnight bag for Lorraine who was blissfully unaware of the arrangements.

Eva Cassidy is playing in the background and the dogs are sleeping. Daisy is curled up by Amanda's feet and the pup, who's already been named around twenty times, has collapsed on the rug in front of the fireplace.

"Ron, will you open the patio doors a bit please? I feel like I'm chain-smoking with all this smoke." Amanda has a valid point; the room is thick with fog and will need a good airing tomorrow.

I get up to open the sliding door a little, aware that my vision is slightly blurred and my gait a little unsteady. I'm going to have a killer hangover tomorrow, especially now I've switched to my favourite vintage port.

"Just going to check on Rachel and switch the coffee machine on," I say, intending to go to my office and send a message to Penny. I feel I can make an exception messaging her tonight, since a lot of tonight's success was down to her hard work, and I want to let her know it all went to plan.

"Who's for coffee?" I ask.

Amanda gives me a nod, and Martyn and Meghan both signal they would like one too.

"Do you want a hand?" Meghan says half-heartedly. She looks shattered, and I'm tempted to tell her that her mascara has smudged, making her look like Alice Cooper, but decide against it.

"No, it's fine, I'll manage," I say. I need to wake myself up, and will probably splash my face with cold water while the coffee percolates.

I head down the corridor towards my office. It's tucked away at the far end of our house, away from any disturbances and is my hidey hole where I can work or have some quiet time to myself. It's also where I keep our safe and the hub for our alarm system with cameras to check in on the main rooms in the house and the garden. I may quickly play it back and watch everyone arriving.

The office is panelled in dark oak from floor to ceiling and, despite having a small window, needs lighting during the day too. They say a bright room is good for inspiration, but I like the cosiness of a dimly-lit room. I rarely use the main overhead light, and certainly can't cope with it right now. I ease myself behind the desk, reaching for my mobile in my pocket. Penny is probably asleep, but at least I know she'll receive my message first thing in the morning.

As I position myself to sit down on the black leather chair, I press the switch on the lamp.

165

My heart freezes.

Every hair on my body stands on end and I let out a gasp.

"Don't make any noise, stay calm and you won't be hurt."

There's a hooded figure in the dark corner of the room and I'm staring straight down the barrel of a sawn-off shotgun.

Chapter 18

RONNIE

In the split second I realise I have a gun pointed at me, I feel winded. My heart misses a beat, and my breathing stops, my chest feels as though it's carrying a ten-ton weight. The transition from inebriated to completely sober feels like a rollercoaster at full speed coming out of a corkscrew turn.

The man is wearing a black polo neck, balaclava and leather gloves and grips the gun with both hands.

"Stand up slowly and move towards the door," he says, his voice low and gravelly.

My brain has frozen, but somehow I automatically follow his command, slowly moving to the door, edging my hands up in the air to appease him and show that I'm at his mercy.

"What is it you want?" I ask, registering that I've probably interrupted him searching for the safe in my office.

"Don't ask questions, just do as I say." He nudges the gun in my direction. "Walk, slowly, keep your hands in the air. Nice and easy."

I have my back to him and follow his command. I can feel the blood pumping furiously through my body, my ears ringing. As I start to walk, he follows, and I can feel the gun pushing into my back.

What's going on? Why is he leading me away from the office?

My stomach lurches as it registers where we're going. We're heading back towards the lounge. With each step, my brain calms a little, and logic starts to vie for authority. This must be a joke, right? Someone has set this up and wants to make a complete prat of me. Payback for all the jokes I've played over the years. Well, this is beyond the pale. Not funny at all. I could quite easily have just had a heart attack back there in my office, dropped down dead with the shock. When I find out who's behind this, there will be hell to pay.

The only sound coming from the lounge is Daisy barking. She must sense that something's wrong, but why isn't anyone talking? I can't hear Amanda calming Daisy down or telling her to be quiet.

I open the lounge doors and enter the room to be greeted by the sight of another man wearing a matching balaclava and holding a pistol in the direction of Amanda, James, and our guests. They're like cardboard cut-outs seated in a semicircle around the corner settee by the glass coffee table. Their eyes immediately turn to me and before I can register what's happening the man behind me shouts.

"Grab the dogs and take them to the kitchen." He is obviously perturbed by Daisy, who is making a terrible job of sounding aggressive, and the pup, who is bouncing around blissfully unaware of any danger.

"Come on, Daisy," I say, grabbing her by the collar as she approaches me. I pat her on the head, barely feeling her smooth silk fur, and command her to follow me. I pick the puppy up in my arms, with the pressure of a gun permanently nudging me in the back. Staring straight ahead, I am slowly paraded out of the lounge and marched towards the kitchen. My mind is working overtime. Why was he waiting in my office? Whoever set this up has really gone to town; how did they arrange *two* actors to come out in the early hours of the morning to try and scare me?

There's a box of Bonios on the kitchen island. I take one and throw it to the ground, telling Daisy she's a good girl. I always knew she'd make a crap guard dog. Chocolate Labs are at the bottom of the pecking order when it comes to intelligence; hardest to train, soft as mud, and whilst Daisy usually alerts us when the postman or delivery man comes to the door, she seems to have completely missed the entrance of these two brutes. Well, at least, I presume there are only two… what if there are more of them?

"Were you at the party?" I ask, quizzing him so that I can hear his voice.

"Shut the fuck up and do as I say."

Whoa! He's aggressive. I certainly don't recognise the voice, and his hooded grey eyes don't look familiar to me.

169

It dawns on me that they probably arrived with the rest of the guests. Of course! They would have mingled with the crowds coming in, blending in unnoticed, before sneaking off to hide out and wait for the right opportunity. I'm certain if I watch the CCTV back, I'll see them strolling in with the party guests.

My thoughts are interrupted as I'm nudged in the back and told to return to the lounge where I'm ordered to sit back down with the others. Amanda has terror in her eyes which sends a tingle up my spine. Her wide-eyed glare also tells me she's confused, her face almost pleading with me.

"Ron, if this is one of your –" She's interrupted before she can finish her sentence.

"Shut up. I don't want to hear a sound out of any of you," the big guy barks at her like an army commander.

"That way, nobody will get hurt and we'll be out of your hair before you know it," the other guy adds as an afterthought. He's softer spoken and slimmer than my abductor. At around six foot, he has a slight build, almost lanky, also wearing black gloves, but holding a pistol which he waves slowly from side to side, pointing towards each of us in turn.

My heart suddenly races with the thought that perhaps this isn't a hoax after all. I can't imagine anyone wanting to end the evening for Amanda in this way, but there has to be some explanation. Panic starts to flood through my veins again.

It's strange how the room appears brighter when you're in shock, things seem clearer as though someone has pressed the high-definition button. I notice the dark knots on the teak tree stump that holds the large circular piece of glass with our drinks on. I know without checking how many glasses are on the table and what is in each. Maybe it's nature's way of preparing you to recall the events for the police investigation later. I notice the brightly-coloured paper strands of party poppers trodden into the deep pile carpet beside Meghan's patent heels. The marble ashtray on the coffee table seems twice its usual size and I can smell the remnants of its contents, which are now mixed with fear.

I'm sitting next to James, and the silence in the room feels like an awkward pause in the middle of a concerto, the moment when you're not sure whether to clap or not. I look at James, who throws me a sideways glance before looking back at our captors, fixing his eyes on the pistol. Could this be him? Could James have set this up? Surely, he wouldn't choose his own mother's birthday to pull such a prank? But then, he could have told her while I was out of the room, prepared her for what was coming.

No. I decide not, Amanda looks genuinely terrified, and I know she's not such a convincing actress. But perhaps he wants revenge for that time we were out at Ray and Lorraine's place in Spain last year. The time I duped him and Rachel with one of my more elaborate pranks. Did I overstep the mark? Rachel's words come flooding back to me. "We'll get you back one day, Ronnie."

We'd been out on Ray's speed boat. Just Ray, Rachel, James, and me. We were on our final water-skiing session before our departure the next day, while our wives were on a shopping spree in Marbella. Ray and I took it in turns to drive the boat whilst the other skied. It was a calm day, not too many other boats around, and the sea had a slight swell, but it was still a smooth ride in his Sea Ray deck boat. We were all thoroughly exhausted, our T-shirts sticking to our wet bodies and Rachel – who doesn't ski – was wearing shorts and her stripey string bikini. I can see it as if it were yesterday.

Before we headed back to shore, James asked if he could take the helm, and Ray agreed. His face was a picture as the wind blew his hair from his face, grinning from ear to ear as he gently upped the power and got a feel for things.

"Don't take it above eighteen knots, and give a wide berth to any other boats," Ray said, as he came to join me at the back of the boat.

The back end sat low in the water and I was perched on the side, holding on to the metal bar. The saltwater splashed against my skin, and I was mesmerised by the foamy wake, until… the little devil popped into my head again.

I leant over to Ray and told him my plan. His nod told me he was in. I waited for a minute or so, looking at

Rachel and James's backs. Rachel had her hand on the rim of the front windshield, standing next to James who was seated on the captain's chair. I nodded my head to signal to Ray, and then let myself drop backwards into the speeding water with any splash disguised by the noise of the engine. My entire wellbeing was entrusted to Ray, but I knew what a great sense of direction he has, and he would have clocked the exact spot where I made my exit. I later learnt that he went to join Rachel and James at the helm and, thankfully, he didn't have to nudge things along.

Less than a minute later, by complete chance, Rachel turned to look at the back of the boat, and on seeing I wasn't there, shouted, "Where the fuck is Ronnie?"

Apparently, James was panic stricken. Ray calmly took control of the situation and guided James to turn the boat around, assuring them that I had been there only a matter of seconds before, so I must have fallen off somehow.

Meanwhile, I was treading water when I saw the boat coming back in my direction. I was glad it hadn't quite gone out of sight since I didn't have a lifejacket on and was aware this could have gone horribly wrong. We were too far from shore for me to swim, but that only made it more exciting. It was the element of risk that made this such a great joke. You must be prepared to go that extra bit further to make something more convincing.

As the boat drew closer, I was aware it wasn't long before they would spot me. The familiar mix of nerves and excitement filled my stomach. Did they believe they had inadvertently caused some catastrophe to happen? Were they scared they wouldn't be able to find me?

I decided at the last minute to finish off my hoax with one final act of glory. Putting my face into the water, I floated on the surface as if unconscious. I could hear the engine slowing as it approached, and then Rachel's screams.

"You've killed your father, you've bloody killed him!" She was hysterical.

I popped my head up and exploded, laughing until my tears mixed with the salt water. The boat cut its engine and glided towards me. Ray lowered the ladder down off the back ramp and helped me aboard. James was furious, cursing like a good 'un whilst Ray and I sat on the back seat, laughing. James looked pretty shaken up, if I'm honest, but after I apologised that familiar smile soon edged its way back onto his face.

Rachel, embarrassed by her reaction, hugged me. "Shit, Ronnie, I thought we'd lost you," she said.

Now I come to think of it, it was a bit mean. You never quite know how a big prank is going to pan out, and in that split second, I imagine James feeling a fraction of what I'm feeling right now. His senses jolted, held in suspension until the moment he realised it was all just a practical joke.

Chapter 19

JAMES

My head is thumping, despite only having had one glass of bubbly. The glass of port, which Dad insisted on, is on the glass table untouched. The sound of everyone's voices seems slightly exaggerated, like someone has turned up the volume for the hard of hearing. I'm the outsider looking in again. Mum and her friends look a little worse for wear, pissed on champagne and cuddled up on the sofa giggling about something.

I'm on the brink of going to find Dad and tell him that I *do* want a coffee after all, when the patio door slides open and a masked intruder bursts in waving a revolver.

"Stay calm, and nobody will get hurt," he says, dropping a large holdall on the floor before approaching us.

I glance across to Mum and the others, and I'm dumbfounded by what I see. All of them are thunderstruck, frozen expressions on their faces as if they've just stepped into a horror scene. Martyn has the wide-eyed look of a deer that unsettles me – he's not one to be easily scared. Mum is clutching Meghan's arm who is shaking like she's cold or something, and Ray, well, I've never seen an expression like that on his face before; it's a mix of confusion and fear, and I can sense the distress emanating from his wheezy breath.

I want to laugh, but push the urge down as I gulp the saliva in my mouth. I rub my tongue around my teeth, my stomach knotted as I appear to be the only one who knows what is going on here. This has got to be hoax of the century. Nobody is going to believe Dad would do this on Mum's birthday, that he could pull off such a wonderful surprise with her extravagant party and then follow it up with a grandiose hold-up. It's like the St Clements drink gag of his. It would be a double whammy, beyond the realms of credibility. Play one surprise straight on top of another, and nobody would suspect it to be real.

I watch as Dad comes back into the lounge with another masked gunman prodding a sawn-off shotgun in his back. I try my best not to laugh. His face is filled with confusion and horror as he looks around at us all, totally lost for words, and I sense one of my flashbacks coming on. Have I not mentioned the flashbacks? They occur regularly, and I'm accustomed to them in the same way I'm accustomed to fixing my poker face when I'm not happy. Some are clearer than others, but when they happen, it's like my nightmares jump into my waking thoughts.

176

Rachel woke me up again last night, telling me I'd had another nightmare, my pillow damp with sweat. I couldn't have recalled the dream this morning had you asked me, but for some reason, I can now feel it starting to emerge in my head. I can hear the distant sound of bells; it's a tune I recognise but can't quite put my finger on it.

Lucas encourages me to talk about my dreams, it gives him the opportunity to say I have unresolved issues from childhood again, and that understanding them could unlock the reason why the dark moods that come over me can be all-consuming. I daren't tell him how my dreams or childhood memories manifest in my daytime thoughts; how they jump into action and trigger me as if I'm experiencing them in my present reality.

Despite my insistence that the only reason I need counselling is to talk about the boating incident at Ray and Lorraine's last year, Lucas always seems far more interested in my childhood experiences and my relationship with Dad. I'm fed up with telling him I don't want to talk about it. That, despite the darker side of some of Dad's jokes, he meant nothing by them, because he always owned up or put things right after having his fun. But then Lucas told me how a child's mind can't differentiate between reality and non-reality until the age of fourteen. That theory is blown by the fact I was exactly fourteen when the school fire alarm went off, and I briefly lost touch with reality, with zero awareness. But he insisted on explaining the theory anyway, relating it to my phobia of dwarves, which is wholly inappropriate in today's world, I know.

When I first saw a dwarf it scared the shit out of me, mainly because Mum had told me that fairy tales and monsters weren't real. Apparently it was all make-believe, and yet, here was living proof that dwarves did in fact live in the real world. Lucas explained how it's not so much that I'm scared of the dwarf, or even its six siblings, but rather what they represent. If *they* are in the real world, it sent me the covert message that so were dragons and monsters, and other horrors that I was exposed to in the so-called 'fictional' world of children. It blew my mind when he explained this, and it made sense.

Lucas asked me to tell him what kind of films scared me as a child, since they could replay in my dreams, and I couldn't think of a single one. Now, however, the thought of last night's nightmare keeps intruding and the tune ringing in my head makes me feel like I'm in the dream again.

I was ten years old, and Dad had allowed me to stay up late to watch a scary film with him.

"Ronnie, you'll give him nightmares," Mum said, and she was right. It still clearly does.

Watching *The Exorcist* at just ten years of age wasn't the best of ideas. Despite it being over twenty years old, Dad insisted I had to watch the three films in order which annoyed me since I had wanted to watch the *Exorcist III* that night, which had been released the year before I was born. He went and found the first film, which initially I found not too dissimilar to the old classic *Omen* – which I do admit, did scare me just a little. But there was something safe about being scared by horror films on the TV; you knew you could switch it off if it became too upsetting, or you could leave the room and go and do something else.

Dad insisted, like always, on turning the lights off for maximum spookiness, and I was grateful, since he couldn't see just how scared I was that night. The intensity began to increase and part of me wanted to tell him to switch the film off halfway through, tell him I was tired and wanted to go to bed, but part of me didn't want him to know I was a wimp and that it had got the better of me. I was strangely drawn to keep watching, hoping to see things resolve – a bit like Dad's jokes, reaching the moment of climax with heart-thumping horror, for him to reveal his hand and make it all safe again.

The music had me clenching my hands and biting my lip. How do horror films know just how to find the right track? Chilling music that has your heart racing and your stomach lurching as you wait for the next scene to emerge. The theme music often haunts me with its repetitive tune that creates the world's worst earworm. It's what's ringing in my ears right now. Mike Oldfield's 'Tubular Bells'.

After kissing Dad goodnight, I went straight to bed, Mum having gone to bed an hour or so earlier. I didn't fancy cleaning my teeth, I just wanted to tuck myself safely under my Pokémon duvet and will myself to sleep to forget all about the film I had just watched.

I switched on my bedside lamp, feeling spooked by the shadows on my wardrobe from the hallway light. Part of me wanted to run into Mum's room and ask for a hug. I needed her reassurance to bring me back to reality after what I'd just seen. To think that some evil force could jump into someone's body and control them in such an evil way was utterly terrifying. To watch Regan in her bed as it shook violently before slowly ascending to the ceiling, with the priest scorching her skin with holy water, had nearly made me pee my pants. But I had wanted to pretend I was brave, that this was no different to watching *The Grinch*, or Roald Dahl's *BFG*.

The more I sense Dad wants to see my fear, the more I hide it. Maybe I'm stubborn, but I just wouldn't give him the satisfaction that night. The strange thing is, I saw how edgy he used to get whenever we watched *The Towering Inferno*, which is as old as the hills, and not even scary, but somehow it triggered him. Mum told me it's the reason he invented the Back Up Ladder; the phobia he has of fire and being trapped in a burning building motivated him to prevent it happening to others. But he would practically chain-smoke when he used to sit and watch the film with me. It didn't bother me, I preferred *The Poseidon Adventure;* it was far more exhilarating watching that humungous wave capsize a cruise ship full of stranded passengers.

I couldn't sleep that night after watching *The Exorcist*, so I put my headphones on to listen to my favourite story CD of *Harry Potter and the Philosopher's Stone*. On the brink of sleep, I was suddenly jolted awake. My imagination was playing tricks on me, and I thought I felt the bed move, a sensation like the dream where you fall off a cliff and are jolted awake just before you land. I lay there silently, trying to focus on the words of the story in my ears, when, to my horror, I felt my bed vibrate. Without any doubt, I knew that I hadn't imagined it this time; the bed trembled, and confusion swept over me as the blood rose to my face.

Sitting bolt upright, I removed the headphones and my heart pounded in my ears. "Max, is that you?" I said, but Max didn't appear. I was frozen to the spot. My heart was banging uncontrollably, and unable to withstand the fear a moment longer, I called out to Mum.

At that precise moment, Dad popped his head up from the end of my bed giggling uncontrollably. Thank God! All the missing pieces fell into place. How on earth did I imagine for one split second that the devil had been cast out of Regan's innocent young body and had sprung into mine? That my bed was about to lift off the floor?

I burst into tears, and Dad's face changed instantly.

"I'm so sorry, James," he said, rushing to sit beside me and wrapping his arms around me. "Shh, shh… you'll wake Mum," he whispered. "It was just me playing one of my pranks."

Through the surge of relief came the feeling of shame for being such a wimp. I couldn't let Dad see he had the better of me, so I calmed my sobs and wiped the tears from my face. "It's alright, Dad," I said. "You just woke me up."

"Shhh," he said again, laying me back down and tucking me in. "It's late, and you need to get some sleep now. Sorry if I scared you."

"Will you fetch Max to sleep with me?" I asked, and Dad went to get him. The dog jumped up onto my bed, resting his paw against my chest as he snuggled into me. I felt safe again.

It's ironic that Dad always made such a good job of scaring me, and yet he made me feel safe too. It was as though he was The Joker from Batman but also the Caped Crusader himself, rescuing me at the point where panic would reach its peak. He always made things alright afterwards, and if I'm honest, part of me enjoyed being scared. It was thrilling. The buzz you feel afterwards is like a hit of euphoria. My body would feel weightless, as a gush of warmth infused my body. My chest would feel expansive and there were little spots of sunlight that burst into my vision. The comfort was overwhelming.

As I recall the blissful feeling of comfort, the bells fade and I'm jolted back to another moment in childhood. I have no idea how old I was, but I know it was before I'd watched *The Exorcist*.

"I dare you to go up and see what that noise is," Dad said one day, with the open hatch door to the attic inviting me up the steep metal steps that hooked over the edge.

"No, you go." I couldn't hear any noise. I didn't want to go up there, I knew this was a set-up, and yet I didn't quite know how.

What was lurking up there, in the dark? The unknown is what makes it scary. You know something is coming, but it's invisible. You also know deep down that no harm will come to you, yet there's still a feeling of uncertainty that gets the adrenaline pumping.

The inevitable happened, and I went up the ladder, with Dad coaxing me to go right inside the attic door. As soon as my feet were fully through the hole, he whipped the ladder away, closed the door and switched off the light (the light switch was down in his bedroom). I stood there disorientated, in total darkness, knowing he had caught me, but when I called out to him to turn the light back on, he didn't reply. My heart sped up with the thought that he had just walked away, leaving me up there to find my own way out. I couldn't move. I was terrified that I might miss the joists and tread on the thin boards, putting my leg through a panel and falling straight through the ceiling. I strained to hear if he was still waiting by the light switch, but all I could hear was my own shuddering breaths.

"Dad!"

I was on the point of hysteria when the light suddenly came back on a few minutes later, and relief flooded through my body. Dad opened the hatch. The grin on his

183

face made me furious, even back then. I wanted to get my own back. Give *him* that moment of spine-chilling fear, where he wasn't quite certain whether it was just a game or something far worse.

Chapter 20

RONNIE

"Mobiles on the table – all of you." The big guy moves in closer, keeping his gun pointing in my direction.

Everyone fumbles in their pockets, and Lorraine grabs her phone from her handbag and throws it on the table. Her eyes are wide as saucers, her hand trembling uncontrollably. You can't fake that kind of fear. She appears as unaware of this as Amanda, I decide. This must be a set-up by one of the boys. Whilst my head is spinning with uncertainty, I decide the only thing I can do is play along.

"I don't have mine on me," Amanda says nervously.

"Stand up." The big guy moves towards her and with backup from the smaller guy pointing his gun at us all, he pats her up and down to make sure she's not lying.

I feel a huge surge of anger. How dare he touch my wife! I get up from the sofa and before I can move another muscle, the lanky guy pulls the cock on the revolver and walks towards me. My automatic reaction is to sit straight back down. I can't take the risk that the gun may be loaded.

James shrugs his shoulders when I shoot him an evil glare; his eyes are nervous, darting from side to side if trying to take everything in. If he has set this up, he's surpassing himself with his acting skills.

"Ronnie, phone!" The lanky guy points his gun at my forehead.

They know my name, I now realise. *Is this a mistake?* I wonder. Surely, they wouldn't make it obvious that they know my name if they were professional armed robbers? This has got to be a set-up. But, then again, my name has been in the papers a lot with Back Up Security doing so well. They must have checked me out when they were doing their homework in preparation for this mission.

I place my iPhone down on the smooth glass table, watching Amanda as she retakes her seat. And then it dawns on me.

Rachel isn't in the room.

I think back to how Rachel has been quieter than usual this evening; it seems so out of character. Is it possible that she has been covertly preparing this mega hoax? Has she been planning this grand hold-up whilst I was planning the surprise party? I look at the dark windows, imagining her outside, watching. When is she going to burst through the patio doors in fits of giggles at her triumph? How long is she going to hold out on this?

James tosses his mobile phone on the glass table. Without thinking, the words blurt from my mouth. "Did Rachel put you up to this?" I try to catch his eye but

James merely shakes his head. He's about to respond when the big guy interrupts,

"Who's Rachel?"

"My fiancée," James replies, giving me a hostile look that I've never seen before.

"And where is she?" The masked assailant's eyes pierce through the peepholes of the balaclava, glaring directly at James.

"Er." He stutters a little. "She went home earlier." *Great acting*, I think, a mix of confusion holding me hostage.

"What, she left without you?" It's clear he doesn't believe James and I realise that if this isn't a hoax, I've put both my son and daughter-in-law in possible danger, but I'm convinced either Rachel or James is behind this. Perhaps they're even in it together.

"She went to bed early with a headache," I say, and James jabs me in my ribs with his elbow.

It's hard to explain what the brain does in this place of confusion that I'm experiencing. The only fragment of calm that I can hang on to is that Rachel or James have set this up, but my brain equally doesn't want to make assumptions or take any risks. I can't bring myself to stand up and put an end to things since my sixth sense tells me that when someone is pointing a gun at me and telling me to be quiet, I could be playing a game of Russian Roulette if I choose to confront them.

"Go take a look around the place, I might have missed something," the big guy says, instructing his accomplice to search the house.

We all sit staring at each other, unable to speak. I sense James's eyes burning into me, his knee jigging up and down nervously. Everyone else has their eyes fixed on the gunman and they look like waxwork dummies with their frozen expressions.

What seems like moments later, a tormented scream comes from upstairs.

James jumps up from his seat, wanting to go to his fiancée, but our captor steps forwards, shouting at him to sit down. James remains standing and turns to face me. What the hell is he playing at? I may be confused right now, unable to gauge what the hell is going on here, but I'm sure of one thing... that scream was genuine.

"Alright, enough, Dad. This isn't funny anymore. Rachel's pregnant."

Chapter 21

JAMES

My heart has never felt so full as the moment when Rachel told me she was pregnant with our first child. She had a look of apprehension, since it's a little sooner than we had planned, and she was worried she'd spoilt the plans for our big day.

"We'll get married after the baby, this is far more important," I said, grabbing her in a tight embrace. "I love you, Rachel, and you're going to be the best mum ever."

I can't wait to be a dad. My whole life I've felt lonely, and struggled to work out what my purpose is in this world. We tick along on the conveyor belt of life, doing well at school to earn our place at college. Then we reach for high grades in sixth form to win a place at university (although I rebelled against this part), and fulfil our parents' dreams, until finally we find a job, which (in my case), feels like you're forcing yourself like a square peg into a round hole.

But hearing I was going to be a dad, everything slotted into place. I knew in that precise moment when Rachel announced the news that this was my purpose, and that my life was finally aligning as it should be.

This child, be it a girl or boy, is going to be so loved, and will be given everything they could possibly need to make them feel whole. Yes, I have every intention of spoiling them – but not with the luxuries that I've been given, rather with time and effort. I want to be there at their first nativity, sports day, football matches. I want to help arrange their birthday parties and take the time to get to know their friends from school, help them with their homework. I know Mum was always standing on the side-lines, like some loyal mascot, but just like Dad with his interests, she was always trying to encourage me to ride bloody horses, do things her way.

I've always sensed, since I gave up riding, that Mum is disappointed with me, that I've offended a part of her that is at the root of all her expectations. It was made worse by the fact that she would always choose her damn horses over me, leaving me to rattle around in our big house all alone, whilst she was out pampering them and paying me off like some stablehand with cakes left in the kitchen, and a new pile of PlayStation games to keep me out of trouble.

Dad was absent too, keeping his hand in with the next big business venture and sauntering off to wherever it is that he goes to. Wherever it was, I always sensed it was more important than staying at home with me. Two parents left me at home, most often with just Max as my companion.

I don't deny that Mum and I have a special bond. Despite my jealousy of her horses, we seem to have grown closer since Rachel came on the scene, and unlike Dad, she openly tells me that she loves me, and is never shy of physical affection. But she doesn't know the real me. She prides herself on how I'm following in Dad's footsteps, but it hasn't crossed her mind that I don't want to be like him. I don't want all the trappings of money and wealth and the adoration of a workforce that bow before me like I'm some bloody emperor. I want a simple, secure life, with warmth and laughter and the safety of my own family in a home with no unexpected surprises around every corner.

Everyone has been asking why Rachel and I have postponed the wedding, and it's been increasingly difficult to come up with convincing excuses. If it had been down to me, I would have told Mum and Dad straight away; I wanted to tell the world, sing it from the rooftops. But this is about Rachel. She has struggled with queasiness and headaches and is convinced that she will jinx things if we tell people too soon, so I've agreed to do it her way. I've been holding the biggest secret of my life for just over five weeks, and I've managed to not let an inkling of my excitement show outwardly.

But my big announcement is ruined. Splattered like a dead bug on a windscreen with the car being driven by Dad.

I was quite happy to play along with Dad's grand hoax, pretend that we're all sitting in some threatening hostage situation, but then he goes and takes it a step too far. I didn't want Rachel upset or anxious in her condition, and things were fine so long as she was tucked up safely in bed. But then he decides to go and involve her, telling the two Krankies whom he's set up as gangsters, that she's asleep upstairs. No doubt he wants her present, to impress her with his crowning act of heroism when he singlehandedly saves us all from the masked intruders.

The familiar feeling overwhelms me. I can't actually believe that Dad went through with allowing the guy to go and wake Rachel up. As her scream echoes down the stairs, I'm struck by the horrific image of her opening her eyes in the dimly-lit bedroom to be greeted by the long barrel of some big idiot's shotgun in her face. Her bloodcurdling scream will remain forever fixed in my mind. It stirs something in me that is indescribable. A part of me wakes up that I had never known was sleeping.

Whether this is a prank that's got out of hand or not, and whether Dad intended the guy to go and find her or not, I will never forgive him for frightening her like this. The shock could have a detrimental effect on her and our baby. I want to go and protect her, tell her that everything is alright, but I can't. As I jump to my feet, I freeze. My legs feel like lead and I'm fixed to the spot.

Chapter 22

RONNIE

My mouth drops open.

Shit! That was why Rachel wasn't drinking tonight, why she had a headache. My boy, and my beautiful daughter-in-law are going to give us a grandchild. I can barely manage to speak as our captor shoves James back down on the sofa, landing next to me. I put my arm out to reassure him, but he flings it away. This can't be him after all; I know him well enough to know that he wouldn't do anything to endanger Rachel, especially if she's carrying his child.

I am racked with guilt. Me and my stupid big mouth. If I hadn't announced that Rachel was upstairs sleeping, she would have been left out of this. I put my head in my hands as it dawns on me that I have just put my son and future daughter-in-law in great danger, but worse still, my future grandchild.

As Rachel shuffles her way into the lounge with a gun pointed at her head, she has a terrified expression on her face that confirms she is not behind this. She's shaking from head to toe, her mouth slightly ajar as she catches at the air for breath. If she looked pale earlier, she looks positively anaemic now. I feel crushed as I watch her take her place on the sofa between Amanda and Meghan, wanting to hug her and tell her it will all be okay.

To think that she's carrying my grandchild.

It overwhelms me with a fatherly protectiveness that consumes me. It makes sense now, why she and James postponed the wedding plans; they clearly want to concentrate on having their first baby together before getting married.

I take in the view of the two most important women in my life. Rachel, whose teeth are chattering as if she's cold, and Amanda, wrapping her arm around Rachel to give some sense of safety. Rachel's wide eyes are blinking furiously, as if she's still trying to wake herself up from a nightmare. Amanda is desperately trying to calm herself and be brave for Rachel. She keeps looking at James, the maternal streak clearly desperate to protect him too; she seems to have aged another forty years in the last ten minutes. As I sit in silence staring at the two most beautiful women I know, on the verge of falling apart, I feel helpless.

"Right," the big guy says in a voice that seems far more confident than the other guy.

I try to imagine his face under the mask. His eyes are dark and sinister, and I can just make out a few creases, which tells me he isn't particularly young. I imagine him to have a beard and perhaps dark brown wavy hair. It's amazing how much we take for granted, determining a person based on their appearance. But only having a blank canvas to work with, makes it so difficult. I'm forced to read his body language, and assess whether this guy's for real, whether he's truly dangerous or just pretending to be.

"Place all your jewellery on the table. Women, earrings, necklaces, bracelets *and* rings. Men, watches and rings."

We all look at each other suspiciously. Amanda stares accusingly at me and I mouth the words, *This isn't me!* I wish it was. I nod at Meghan and Lorraine to signal that they should co-operate, and I'm overwhelmed with shame. This is all my fault, whether it should turn out to be a hoax or not. This is my home, with a fancy all-singing, all-dancing security system, and yet I have failed to keep them safe.

"Now!" He points the gun closer towards Amanda, who lets out a small gasp.

The jangle of various items of jewellery reverberates on the glass as we all place our items obediently on the table like naughty schoolchildren handing over hidden sweets. Meghan has the most to remove; she's adorned with gold jewelled rings, a thick gold necklace and a pair of diamond drop earrings which I dearly hope are not real. She bites her lip as she places them carefully on the coffee table, and I take in every inch of her, trying to assess whether perhaps she and Martyn are behind this. Her makeup has streaked down her face, her curls have dropped into a mass of tangled frizz and I've never seen

195

her look so rough; it's like a scene from *The Rocky Horror Show*. She barely blinks and her face is contorted with fear. It's no use, my stomach tightens as I watch Martyn trying to reassure her by squeezing his arm tighter around her shoulders. This isn't them.

James is ordered to remove his Rolex watch that I bought for his twenty-first birthday, and I'm shocked by his refusal. He sits beside me with his head bowed, playing with its clasp.

"On the table, now!" The big guy is clearly running out of patience and to my horror James stares him in the eye and says,

"And what if I don't?"

I don't understand, it's not like him to display such blatant heroics and I feel a sense of panic that he's putting us all in immediate danger. Surely he doesn't want to do anything to jeopardise the safety of Rachel and the baby?

And then it dawns on me.

There's only one explanation as to why he would react like this, and I realise that it's me. He thinks that this whole set-up has been orchestrated by me. I'm filled with horror and try to whisper something to him, but Rachel starts crying.

"James, do as he says."

Amanda pulls her in closer, and I'm relieved that Rachel's despondency has the desired effect and James begins to unfasten his watch. I feel a tug of guilt as I watch it take its place on the table. I clearly remember his twenty-first birthday and how his face lit up when he finally got to the centre of the large gift box that I had wrapped with dozens of layers to throw him off the scent. He'd been ecstatic. He'd wanted a Rolex watch ever since his eighteenth.

We sit like punished schoolchildren, obeying the head teacher after our misdemeanour. Meghan helps Amanda to remove the tri-colour gold necklace that she has owned for less than twenty-four hours. She places it on the table in a robotic manner, her face expressionless. I remain sitting upright with my elbows on my knees, watching Lorraine and Ray as they remove their treasured items of jewellery. I feel completely impotent as I watch the pile increase with everyone's items.

"Now empty your pockets," the big guy says.

I fumble in my trouser pockets and remove a packet of Marlboro which I place on the table. God, I need a cigarette. My Dunhill lighter is on the bar by Amanda's presents, but for some reason, they don't seem interested in investigating that part of the room, and I have a feeling I know what the answer would be if I ask to have a smoke.

The table is now covered in random paraphernalia, from a used tissue to car keys, and Martyn's wallet. There is a tiny brown bottle with a yellow label inscribed with the words 'Rescue Remedy' that James has placed on the table and I wonder what the hell it is.

It feels as though we've been violated, stripped not just of our personal items, but our dignity. The

197

disempowerment of being in such a vulnerable position renders us like puppets on their string. They could ask anything of us right now, strip down to our underpants or do an impersonation of a chicken and we would do it. We are totally at their mercy.

The lanky guy sifts through the items on the table, picking out the wallets and items of jewellery as if sifting through a box of Quality Street searching for the big purple one.

The big guy breaks the silence. "Now your handbags." It's an order, not a request. I watch as the lanky guy places the wallets and jewellery in a black leather holdall resting by the sideboard before he returns his focus to us.

Lorraine and Meghan tip the contents of their evening bags onto the table, and amidst tampons, lipsticks and hairbrushes, there is little of any value. The lanky captor grabs a gold compact and a couple of crumpled notes, which he adds to his leather holdall. It strikes me that it's a blessing how dainty women's evening bags are, barely accommodating more than some touch-up makeup, a few tissues and a hairbrush.

The sound of Daisy whimpering penetrates the silence, and Amanda and I look at each other. Daisy's barely had a chance to get to know the new pup, and being stranded in the kitchen alone with him is clearly bothering her. It's the least of our worries right now, but Amanda speaks up.

"The dogs need to be let out." She looks nervously at the big guy.

The two captors look at each other. The big guy nods at the smaller guy. "You take her. Do a sweep of downstairs with her and then report back," he says.

My heart is pounding.

Please, God, no. Don't take my wife out of my line of sight.

"Take me with her." My words sound like a question, pleading to let me accompany them, for fear that Amanda may be hurt. Is there some ulterior motive here? What if he were to sexually assault her at gunpoint? Or worse, shoot her to prove to us all that this is no game?

But something is bugging me; why haven't they asked me where the safe is? Surely, they know in a house this size that I have a safe. Wasn't that why the big guy was hanging out in my study?

"Take me," I say again.

"Stay where you are," he says. "And behave yourself. That way, she won't get hurt."

I watch as Amanda is marched out of the room at gunpoint by the lanky guy. I'm glad it's him and not the other one, since I sense he's less of a threat. He seems nervous, a little edgy, as if either this isn't going as planned, or this is his first time doing a hold-up. But either way there's still danger, more so with the latter, since with less experience, there's more room for mistakes. If he gets scared or is forced into a corner, perhaps he'll press that trigger without understanding the full extent of what damage it will cause.

As they leave the room to head off towards the kitchen, I pray that Amanda doesn't put herself at risk.

There's a panic button installed under one of the kitchen units which alerts the police station if we have a situation. But whilst I want her to find an opportunity to press it, I'm equally scared that she may jeopardise her safety. It's why I wanted to go with them. Anything I can do to help I will; I want my wife and son, all my friends, to get to safety and if anyone is going to take any risks, it needs to be me.

Rachel continues to sniffle. She looks across at James with a pained expression, and I realise that she's not just thinking of herself and James – she's thinking of the precious life inside her. I move my hand to rest on James's knee to reassure him, but he flicks it away like he's swatting a fly.

The silence is painful. I strain to hear any sounds coming from the kitchen, any signs that Amanda is struggling. The years of our marriage flood my thoughts and I feel another stab of guilt as I ponder whether I've been a good enough husband to her. I know I can be a bit selfish at times, but I've always convinced myself that she's happy so long as she's kept by me and has her horses to tend. But I should have shown more interest in her, perhaps listened to her suggestions rather than forcing mine on her. I should have included her in more things that I do in life and spent less time down the club or seeing Penny, and more time at home with her.

"Look, just take what you want, and don't hurt us." Lorraine's voice is surprisingly calm. "Ronnie will give you the code to the safe, won't you, Ronnie?"

I'm surprised by her outburst.

Before I can respond she continues, "Please. Take what you've got, and we promise not to call the police."

Why did she say that? Why would she offer up my safe?

My head starts spinning with confusion again. Could it be that *she* arranged this somehow, but it's not going as she planned? Does she realise that she's gone too far now that we've discovered Rachel and James are expecting, and wants to signal to the guys to wrap things up?

"Shut up," Big Guy says. "We'll get to the safe when we're good and ready."

I ponder at the bravery of Lorraine's attempt, how she seems to speak on behalf of all of us. Her demeanour appears far too composed.

In the eternal wait for Amanda to return, I find my mind springing back to the convincing performance Lorraine gave at the dinner table tonight. Her acting skills were magnificent when she asked for the second St Clements. Could she be acting now? If so, it's a prime example of a joke that's gone badly wrong. If this is her, it would seem she didn't trust the others to be let in on the joke, and she's certainly employed some truly great actors, because I'm usually good at reading people and situations, but I can't work this one out. My eyes remain fixed on her as the memory floods back to the time I played my best joke on her, which now feels like it was probably my worst.

We were in Ray and Lorraine's penthouse in Malaga. It was the summer of 2012 and everyone had gone to bed, apart from Lorraine and Amanda who wanted to stay up and watch a horror film together. We left them to watch *Nightmare on Elm Street* and the horrors of Freddie Kruger, a film I had seen over a decade earlier and had no interest in watching again.

An hour or so later, I was unable to sleep, despite reading my Tom Clancy novel. I started to daydream, and a picture came to my mind. I couldn't get it out of my head – it was brilliant. Another opportunity for a practical joke, if only I could find the right materials.

The first thing I needed was a glove, and whilst the penthouse apartment was bordered with planters and a dozen or so ceramic flowerpots, I doubted Ray would possess such a thing as a gardening glove. He was audibly snoring in the room next to ours, and I wasn't going to wake him to ask, so I needed to find some other substitute.

Padding quietly along the corridor, I opened the large cloaks cupboard in the hallway, easing the door open slowly in case it should creak. It contained an array of coats, umbrellas, shoes, and an abandoned mop. I reached up to the top shelf where I could see Ray's baseball cap and a woollen scarf. As I fumbled around, the perfect object tumbled down and hit my face. Ray's ski glove! He'd told me he'd driven to Sierra Nevada last season which is only about a three-hour drive, and the skiing was pretty good, he'd said. I'm not convinced though, it can't be as good as the Alps.

The glove was perfect for my needs, and a few seconds later, I'd located the second one and tucked them both down the front of my pyjamas as I headed towards the kitchen, creeping past the TV room since the door was slightly ajar.

The kitchen had just enough light from the hallway for me to find the cutlery drawer without switching the light on. I was just pulling the drawer open when the overhead light switched on, dazzling me as my eyes tried to readjust.

Amanda gasped.

"Christ, you scared me," she said. "What are you doing?"

"Nothing," I lied, closing the drawer and reaching for a glass from the overhead cabinet. "Just need a glass of water."

"If you're sneaking around for midnight snacks in the fridge again, you'll be the one who's sorry when you stand on the scales when we get home."

"No, not me. Honestly, hon."

I stood and drank my water, while she fetched a packet of chocolate biscuits from the cupboard.

"Hypocrite," I said as she left the kitchen.

"Night," she replied, trailing off to the lounge.

With the coast clear, I carried out my task and grabbed five steak knives from the drawer. Holding them behind my back, I carefully sneaked back to my bedroom where I carried out my preparations.

The gloves were mainly black, with some grey piping, and I carefully pierced each knife through the tip of each finger. Thankfully, there was just enough room to squeeze my hand in alongside the wooden handles, and I could feel the hard lumpy wood pressing into my fingers. The sparkling metal of the ridged knives jutted out of the fingertips of the glove – it was perfect. I decided it wasn't necessary to use the second glove, one hand would be enough.

I switched the bedroom light off before sliding open the patio door that led out to the terrace from our room. The tiles felt cold under my feet, and the heat of the Mediterranean sunshine had been replaced by a cool breeze that brought goosebumps to the surface of my arms. There were a few stars punctuating the black velvet sky, but the moon was eclipsed by a series of clouds, giving it a dramatic, unearthly appearance.

My heart was thumping as I lingered outside the lounge patio doors. I didn't need to place my ear against the glass, since the door was slightly open, and I could clearly hear the TV. I positioned myself in front of the gap, the curtain moving slightly in the breeze. I could barely breathe with the excitement of scaring the girls with my chilling re-enactment of Freddy Kruger. But I wanted to time it right.

"Oh my God!" The gasps of horror echoed from the room as they watched the climax of the film.

"I can't watch, I can't watch." I imagined Amanda curling herself in a tight ball on the sofa, peeking out from behind a cushion.

The music finally signalled that the credits were rolling.

"I don't think I'll be able to sleep after that," Amanda said.

"It's seriously freaked me out, I'm going to have nightmares for sure," Lorraine said.

My first attempt of scraping the knife tips down the window went unnoticed. But once Lorraine had turned off the TV, the rasping sound became clearer. It was difficult to contain my laughter; part of me wanted to just burst in on them and show them what I was doing.

"What was that?" Lorraine said.

"What?" Amanda replied, clearly not as concerned as Lorraine.

I peeped through the gap in the curtains, the brightness of the lounge keeping me safely hidden in the darkness. They were standing next to each other, Lorraine with the remote still in her hand, looking around the room, terrified, Amanda on the brink of heading towards the lounge door.

I scraped my fingers a little louder.

"That scratching noise!" Lorraine said, the fear brewing nicely in her tone.

Silence followed, and I gave one more scrape against the metal of the door before gently moving the curtain with my gloved hand and letting the tip of metal peep through.

"What the fuck is that?" Amanda said, as she edged closer towards the lounge door, but Lorraine was frozen to the spot.

I placed more of the glove through the curtain, and I really did not expect the hysterics that followed.

"It's a dream, it's a dream!" Lorraine screamed in terror. "I'm in a dream, wake me up, Amanda!"

They both started screaming and I burst through the curtain, half-expecting to see Lorraine standing in a puddle of wee.

As I burst into laughter, Amanda stepped forwards and slapped me square around the face. I deserved it, I guess. They were both scared out of their wits, and in that moment of confusion, they truly believed they were in the film, trapped in a nightmare.

"You arsehole, Ronnie." The relief on Lorraine's face was clear with the colour returning to her cheeks.

"I'll get you back one of these days," Lorraine said, as she gave me a friendly slap on the shoulder before heading off to bed.

Chapter 23

JAMES

I know the moment Rachel walks into the room that things have gone too far. Seeing the one thing that I need to protect, to make safe in my life, forms a feeling inside my stomach that tears at my insides like a dark unnameable force.

Fear starts to pump through my veins like cold ink, my spine begins to tingle and a fog closes in all around me, as though I'm slipping into some other realm. I can still hear voices talking, but I'm no longer a real person, I am not James.

I stare at the glass on the coffee table, seeing the reflection of the chandelier hanging above. Its opulent crystals throw a sparkle across the glass like little jewels that bedazzle my senses. They appear to be moving, evolving into stars which are getting brighter and attempting to blind my vision. As I fix my eyes on the table, the watch that was there just a few seconds ago has vanished, as if pulled into a black hole.

It's no use, I can't hold on. I feel a switch of electrical current inside my head and I'm transported back to school. There's an echo all around me of excited voices and the vague smell of fish pie from the canteen. *God, I hate fish pie!* I feel the rough fibres of my polyester trousers that are too tight for my legs, the discomfort of my school tie which makes me clutch at my neck to try and loosen it.

The shrieks and laughter are bouncing off the walls, coming from above and beneath me. We're on the top floor of the art block at school. I'm fourteen years old and hanging out with a cool group of lads. I feel awkward, knowing as I always do that I don't quite fit in. Maybe I am a little needy sometimes, but the loneliness of being an only child makes my friendships all that more important. The isolation of school holidays, with Christmases spent with just Mum, Dad and my grandparents, always gives me a sense that I'm missing out. Jake says I suffer from FOMO (fear of missing out), but he doesn't know how precious every opportunity is to spend time with him and the others; every moment makes up for all the lonely times when I have nobody to connect with.

We're waiting in the stairwell, leaning against the metal railings that overlook the floor-to-ceiling window panels. Jake and Josh are spitting over the side to see if they can hit someone still ascending the stairs. The expanse of glass in front of me overlooks the playground and science block that seems like a distant Lego building from this height.

I always imagine I'm at the top of a huge skyscraper when we come up here, like the one that was struck on 9/11. The traumatic scenes flash through my mind as I remember sitting and watching events unfold on the TV with Dad just a couple of years ago. He rewound and played the scenes repeatedly, watching people as they jumped out of windows to escape the great fire that swept through the building, and it was the first time I saw my dad cry.

"Turn it off," Mum said. "Enough." But it was like he was obsessed with watching it and I sat there in silent horror, not knowing how to process the atrocities that were shown again and again on the TV screen. It was like watching *The Towering Inferno* only I couldn't comprehend that Dad kept telling me this was real.

I knew what death was, I had been to both of my grandfathers' funerals, and one of Dad's cousins who had died of a brain tumour when I was nine. Dad and I would often talk about death, and that was when I started to become aware of my own mortality. I've been terrified of death ever since, and I can't tell anyone; I'd look stupid, and nobody would understand. Dad's afraid of death too, that's why he always talks to me about it; I think he's trying to make sense of his own mortality.

Whilst the memory of 9/11 has faded with time, it comes flooding back to me standing at the top of the art block, as if I can see through the glass panes with the eyes of one of those poor victims. Just how horrific to throw yourself to your own death, desperate to escape

209

the fumes and smoke and being burnt alive, only to plummet to an equally horrific death. How could it be possible to make that choice?

Mr Loughlin arrives to unlock the art room and as we bunch up to push our way through the dozen or so students in front of us, I stand directly under the fire alarm, which is one of the old-fashioned bright red bells like a huge red apple with a silver core. Suddenly, with no warning, it blasts a cacophonous sound which echoes through the entire stairwell, making me convulse with shock.

"Right, turn around everyone, file down the stairs in an orderly manner." Mr Loughlin directs the crowd before him, back towards the stairs.

Everyone turns in a wave to descend the staircase again. I feel like I've gone deaf, there's a stillness all around me, even though Mollie and her bitchy clique of friends are pushing their way through. One of them, Emma, I think she's called, has secretly started to smile at me when the others aren't around, but she stares at me scornfully, laughing and chatting with the others as they file past me.

"Come on, James, move, you twat!" Josh says, but I'm frozen to the spot. My mind has gone blank, and my limbs don't feel as if they belong to me; they've detached from my body and I can't seem to breathe.

The endless ringing echoes through my ears, the loud noise crashing in on me and transporting me to that office floor in New York. I start to cry, believing that I'm in imminent danger, and yet, I cannot move. My mates scuffle past me with baffled expressions on their faces, to make way for Mr Loughlin who somehow manages to reach me just as the sound ends and the building is silent again.

"It's alright, James, it's just a fire practice," he says. "There's no danger, it's not a real fire." His calming voice activates my senses again, and like an angel, he gently brings me back to the present moment, making me feel safe.

But I'm not.

I notice Mr Loughlin slowly looking down towards my feet and I lower my head to follow the direction of his gaze. The warm feeling that I had thought was blood seeping through my skin just a few seconds ago, is still trickling down my leg to my ankles, but it's not blood. I've wet myself in front of the entire class, and somehow, I feel that this is one nightmare I'll never get over. I feel an overwhelming desire for this to be a video that I can replay again when I get home, one that I can edit so that the whole scene that just happened plays out differently.

"It's okay, James, let's go and get you sorted, lad," Mr Loughlin says. "We can fix this."

Chapter 24

RONNIE

I hear the back door slam in the kitchen, jolting me out of my reverie. Big Guy flinches.

"Everything all right in there?"

I glance at Lorraine for her reaction, and she looks discernibly alarmed. It feels like I have seconds to work this out, to work *her* out.

Before Big Guy gets his reply, Amanda appears at the top of the two steps that lead into the lounge. The lanky guy leaves the double doors ajar and he keeps the gun firmly centred in the middle of her back.

Lorraine judders as she lets out a sigh of relief, and I notice she has tears in her eyes. My confidence that this is her is starting to wane.

"Yeah – we shut the puppy in the utility room with newspaper," Lanky Guy replies. "All sorted."

Amanda rejoins us on the sofa, and I notice beads of sweat on her forehead, her face deathly pale, and her eyes like a cornered rabbit. God, I want to hold her. I feel a weight pushing down on me as if the ceiling is coming down on my shoulders. Why have I been such a dick?

She doesn't deserve a husband who sneaks off to have it away with another woman. The thought of losing her opens my eyes to the fact I could equally lose her if she ever discovers I've been playing away.

The guilt of the past two years engulfs me and I want to vomit. I now know, without a shadow of a doubt, that *if* we get through this, I'm going to end the affair. Penny has to go; she needs to return to being nothing more than a secretary for the company and somehow understand that our time is over. I'll go and see her this week and explain. The game has changed. No more risks. I'll be satisfied with what I've got, which is a beautiful family, and wealth that gives us more than most people could ever wish for. If I get bored, I'll have to learn to handle it. Perhaps find another hobby, or even start to make the effort to join Amanda down at the stables. She'd appreciate that.

"Take him to find his wife's jewellery," the big guy says, signalling towards me.

I stand up, looking at Amanda, and try my best to reassure her. The lanky guy seems surprised at the command and points the gun directly at me; my heart quickens, banging against my chest.

"You heard him. Move!" he says, the gun waving haphazardly.

"Whoa, okay." I stagger slightly, nervous that the thing could go off unintentionally.

I need to keep calm. If we all do as they say, and they get what they want, we can get out of this alive. He said as much, didn't he? It's not the time for any heroics and I look at James, trying to warn him of such. Anything stupid could jeopardize everyone. But James's mouth is tightly set, and I sense by the rigidness of his jaw that he's angry. He seems to be staring straight through me and I feel a wave of concern at his dazed expression.

Something's not right.

All the times I've managed to jump out of joker mode and tell him that everything is alright, that it's safe, and yet, here I am, unable to put things right for him tonight. What the hell must he be thinking?

"Walk," Lanky Guy says.

I look at Lorraine before I leave, and her hunted expression confirms my suspicions that this is definitely not her doing after all. The blood has drained from her face, and her unblinking eyes look glassy. She gives me a pitiful look which tells me to stay safe, and I begin to head out of the lounge, leaving James and my family behind.

"It's upstairs in the bedroom," I say, heading for the huge curved staircase, that seems like a mountain to climb under the circumstances.

As I step on each tread, I contemplate falling backwards, to knock my assailant back down the stairs. But there's the possibility of his gun being loaded and firing straight into my back as I take the fall. My mind cannot compute quick enough; every thought is rushing through my head trying to find a way out, find a solution.

I need to do something while I've got the weaker one alone.

As we reach the top, I remove my hand from the smooth oak handrail. I turn left to head towards our bedroom. He switches the hallway light on behind me to illuminate the way, and I tentatively stop at the entrance to our bedroom.

"Keep going," he says.

I walk through the entrance corridor to our room, and the sensor triggers the floor lights by my feet, guiding my next few steps.

As the full room comes into view, I look out of the leaded windows at the black night. I try to imagine someone on the outside looking in. A neighbour, perhaps. They could rush to call the police and help save us from this situation. But the sad reality is, we're not overlooked. The nearest house is a quarter of a mile up the road. There is nobody out there who has an inkling of our awful dilemma. I've never felt more closed in, as if the house has become an airtight container and we're running out of air.

"Shut the curtains," Lanky Guy says, as he catches me looking out of the window.

I do as I'm told and as I slowly draw the curtains the overhead light comes on when he flicks the main switch. I pause, a sliver of dark window remaining. I catch a glimpse of our reflections and see myself and my attacker, as if watching myself in a movie, our two silhouettes forming the lead roles in the climax of a gangster movie. Then the curtain closes, before it ends.

Lanky Guy's eyes search the room for a sign of where Amanda keeps her jewellery box. Our large sleigh bed is covered with a smooth velvet throw, scatter cushions placed at perfect angles. How I wish me and Amanda were tucked up in it right now, snuggled in safely and allowing this exhaustion to subside into deep sleep.

The digital clock on Amanda's bedside table says it's 2.30 a.m., but it feels as though time has stood still. It feels as if my entire life, both past and potential future, have been sucked into a vortex of this present moment and reality has turned on its head into non-reality. Perhaps this is all just a bad nightmare, one of those lucid dreams where I will suddenly wake up. Or perhaps this is one of those out-of-body experiences and I'm merely passing time before being sucked back into my body, right there, where my side of the bed is perfectly un-crumpled.

"Where is it then?" the lanky guy says.

I'm jolted by his voice, and slowly walk over to Amanda's double pedestal dressing table. Makeup is still scattered over the surface where she glammed herself up just a few hours earlier, blissfully unaware of the party that lay ahead. Blissfully unaware of the chaos that would unfold afterwards.

The soft pink leather jewellery box sits on the table, and I pick it up to offer to him. He nudges the gun towards the bedroom door, indicating he wants me to head back the way we came.

"Look, please, can we talk about this?" I say, trying to stall for time.

"Just walk," he replies, raising the revolver to eye level.

I turn towards the bedroom door, carrying the jewellery box in both hands. I'm confused. Why didn't he check its contents first or ask me to enter our dressing room to search for any more valuables? Amanda keeps her petty offering of valuables hidden in a small jewellery box tucked behind her jumpers on a shelf in the wardrobe; it contains a couple of sentimental items like a brooch that belonged to her mother, and her grandmother's sapphire ring, but I'm not going to offer it up if he's stupid enough not to ask.

As we make the slow journey back towards the staircase, I'm shuffling each foot slowly, desperately trying to think of a way to tackle this guy. I could throw the jewellery box in the air to distract him, but *then* what am I going to do? Even if I manage some spectacular spin and knock the gun out of his hand, what do I do next? I couldn't live with myself if the other guy hurts one of my friends or family. He would surely hear the commotion and then take one of them hostage, threatening to shoot them in the head because of my actions. My brain usually works at breakneck speed; it can calculate risk and rewards of business in a flash, but with the mix of alcohol and tiredness, and the trauma of the whole situation, the cogs just aren't working. Instead, I seem to be reacting with automated obedience.

As I re-enter the lounge everyone has their heads bowed. Amanda raises her eyes briefly and her relief is tangible. The others slowly look up to check I'm okay, all except James. His head remains bowed, his eyes fixed to a certain spot on the coffee table, where his Rolex watch was just a short while ago. It's as though the watch is still sitting there and by keeping his eyes fixed on the spot, he can will it to remain there. He seems a million miles away.

Somebody's mobile phone buzzes in the leather holdall. Our eyes all meet each other for a second, and I wonder if it's Penny. If only I could get a message to her that we need help. She'd know what to do; she'd have armed police all positioned around the property to get us out of this mess. But I have no way to communicate. My watch and my phone have been stripped from me.

"I need the toilet," Rachel whispers to the others.

"Take her," Big Guy says, more interested in opening the jewellery box I've placed on the table.

James looks up and gives his fiancée a look I can't fathom. He doesn't seem to be as fearful as I am at the thought of Rachel leaving the room alone with this guy; he seems resigned to letting her go. On the other hand, I want to go with them, keep her safe.

"Let me take her," I say, trying to keep the desperation from my voice.

The big guy gives me a shove, pushing me in the direction of James.

"Sit back down and shut the fuck up," he says.

I watch impotently as Rachel is marched out of the room at gunpoint, wondering which bathroom she'll lead him to. Will she take him to the downstairs toilet, the one in the gym, or one of the bathrooms upstairs? Will she get the chance to lock herself in, or will he go in with her and watch her?

I'm distracted by Big Guy, who removes the top layer from the jewellery box, and, after tipping out the compartments of earrings and trinkets, pulls out the necklaces and bracelets from the base of the jewellery box. I know he's disappointed, despite not seeing his expression. Amanda has never been big on jewellery. She wears the same understated diamond studs day in and day out, her wedding and engagement ring and a simple Tiffany charm bracelet, which is old-fashioned these days, but she holds on to the sentimentality of it being a twenty-first birthday gift.

The knotted mess of different length necklaces lies messily on the table, clearly costume jewellery, but Big Guy picks out the Tiffany charm bracelet that is heavy with years' worth of trinkets, and shoves it in his pocket. Whilst I know this will upset Amanda, I can't help but think, *Wow, all this for a Tiffany bracelet? Do these guys know what they're doing?* The stereo on the sideboard unit is Bang and Olufsen and worth over five grand, and yet they don't seem to have even noticed it. The Martin

Leighton original hanging over us all may as well be a kid's crayon drawing since neither of them has so much as glanced in its direction. There's something unnerving about all of this, and I can't put my finger on it. It's as if they're acting out the typical bank robber scene, grabbing for jewellery and watches and having fun while keeping us captive with their big boy guns.

Shouts echo from somewhere near the entrance hall. Big Guy straightens up, keeping his eyes on us, but I see the concern – he's pacing, and has tightened his grip on the gun.

He edges closer to the door, keeping his shotgun pointing in our direction.

"Everything alright?"

"She wants me to stand outside the door." The reply is distant, and I know Rachel's chosen the downstairs guest toilet.

"Tell her she gets a fucking bullet through her head if she doesn't comply."

I feel my heart skip a beat and Amanda visibly tenses up, looking at James to try and reassure him, but his eyes are still fixed on the glass table.

"Stand against the door and tell her you'll turn your back if you must," Big Guy yells, but there's no reply, and we can't tell whether his instructions were received.

I have no idea whether its seconds or minutes since Rachel left the room. Time keeps stopping and starting with adrenaline being drip-fed through my veins with moments when I could collapse with exhaustion and others where it surges as if being directly injected. The latter activates my senses, like an animal, perhaps a cat watching its prey and preparing to pounce whilst safeguarding itself from falling victim to a bigger predator, a fox maybe. My head is throbbing and a deep pain behind my right eye tells me I have a migraine threatening. I would guess it's been around an hour and a quarter since they took us captive, and I wonder if they're going to drag this out all night, just for the hell of it.

There's a commotion out in the hallway, and the sound of banging makes us all sit upright. We hear Lanky Guy shouting,

"Open the fucking door before I kick it down and shoot you."

Rachel has found her opportunity to shut herself in, but to what avail? She's got no means to call for help, there's no panic button in the toilet, and not even a window to escape through. The banging increases; the lanky guy's frustration at his mistake is clearly being taken out on the bathroom door.

"Sean, get your skinny arse back in here." The big guy seems really pissed now. He's just given us the name of his accomplice without even noticing. *Sean.* The name conjures up an image of Sean Bean, yet this guy certainly isn't as hardcore, and I can't imagine him playing the honourable leader in *Game of Thrones*.

In the blink of an eye, Sean is back in the room, and changes places with Big Guy who rushes to the locked door. There's a loud explosion of anger as he bellows at Rachel that she has ten seconds to unlock the door and rejoin us all before he kicks it in and shoots her.

As he counts backwards, the tension rises, and I find I'm holding my breath.

His countdown nears the end, and he starts bashing what I imagine to be the handle of his gun against the door. Amanda and Meghan start screaming, unnerving Sean who is waving his gun in their direction. Just as Big Guy says, "Two," we hear movement.

Rachel is crying as Big Guy roughly pushes her back in the room.

"Try a stunt like that again, and both you and your fiancé will get a bullet through the skull, do you hear me?" Rachel nods, as she collapses on the sofa with Amanda who cradles her in her arms as if she's a small child. James has broken from his trance, and makes to lunge towards them, but I place my hand across him, stopping him from rising out of his seat.

"I'm sorry," Rachel whimpers as she nurses her arm where she was manhandled.

"Get the cuffs," Big Guy says. "This one's trouble."

A pair of black metal handcuffs are pulled from the holdall. We watch dumbstruck, as they're snapped around Rachel's delicate pale wrists, shackling her into submission.

"It's okay, Rachel, go along with them, it will all be fine," I say, but she's looking at James who refuses to look back.

I've learnt two things in the last five minutes. Skinny Guy is called Sean, which seems a stupid mistake to reveal to us; either it's a bluff and they aren't using their real names, or it's his birth name, and they've let the cat out of the bag. Secondly, I've been alerted to the fact that they have more than just guns with them, although I can't imagine there are enough handcuffs in that bag for all of us. It's been clear from the outset that the big guy is the one in charge and I find him far more intimidating than his lanky partner. It's slowly dawning on me that if one of these two is going to increase the level of violence, it will be him.

Chapter 25

JAMES

"Do you feel safe now?" My counsellor's voice is echoing round and round in my head. He comes into focus and I can see him sitting in his brown leather armchair, the table between us on which is a box of tissues for clients that may need them, but not me. Crying in public brings shame. It's a sign of weakness and something I take great care not to do in front of others, especially men.

"How did it make you feel?"

Why do counsellors ask so many dumb questions? He's the only person I've talked to in detail about what happened when I was at school. I buried it, or rather my subconscious did, protecting me by safely tucking the whole episode away in a drawer with unmatched socks and Christmas handkerchiefs from Grandma. I'm annoyed he forced me to open it.

How did it make you feel? The words echo in my mind, reverberating through my body. Who wants to remember how something makes you feel when it's the most mortifying experience of your entire life? But the silence is becoming unbearable.

"Like I wanted to scream at my dad."

"And why is that?" he asked.

"Because he wasn't there to make it all better. He was the one who made me watch the footage of 9/11 over and over again. He was the one who made me so scared of death and thinking about how or what may happen when that day may come, and yet he wasn't there when it happened."

"But it didn't happen; you're still here, James."

"Am I?" I said.

It was as though a piece of me died that day at school. My entire self-respect shrivelled up and burnt in the fire of 9/11, leaving charred remnants of myself to face the shame of what was to come. If I'm honest, had I seen a classmate of our age wet his trousers, I think I would have felt pity for him too, but pity comes in different shades. You either take pity on someone and take steps to help them feel better, do what's required to support them and help them get back on their feet again, or you retreat, shunning them with disgust for not being able to get a grip, for not fitting in.

The latter happened, and apart from Robert, I sensed the entire school exploited the event as an opportunity for mockery. I kept my head down, pretending that I wasn't aware of the sniggers and didn't know I was the topic on everyone's lips. My face became a picture of indifference as if I had no idea what the whispering was all about and my invisible forcefield went up.

My work became my outlet. If I threw myself into getting the highest grades that I could, I would show everyone that I was better than them. The jibes I received each time I was praised for my latest A grade making me out as 'teacher's pet' started to transpose the true reason of why people were judging me. I would get straight As in all my subjects and then be too good for this place, too good for these snotty-nosed rich kids.

Mum and Dad said they wanted me to stay at school for sixth form, only because they felt I would get better results, but then Dad said that if I proved myself and gained high grades, they would consider sending me to another college since it showed I was serious about my studies and that I was responsible enough to no longer need the backup of a cosseted private school.

When I finally made it to college, it gave me the opportunity to start afresh. No one knew me and I was no longer 'the boy who peed his pants'.

With a clean slate, I created a new image. Mum and Dad battled with my long hair, and there were many arguments, especially with Dad, but I wanted to lose the preppie look and loved my Dr. Martens and full-length leather jacket with my dark metal-rimmed sunglasses. If it weren't for the long hair that was pulled into a ponytail, I was a dead ringer for Neo from *The Matrix* – my favourite film of all time. I began to feel invincible. Nothing could touch me, and my lack of interaction and banter unwittingly made me into a 'strong and silent' type, something that won me many friendships, especially with girls, who were intrigued by me.

Despite my dad's many accusations that I was gay, I was well aware of my own sexuality, and I was most definitely heterosexual, but I was also intrigued by the openness and sensitivity that girls displayed. Most of the lads I knew were bunking off lessons and driving off somewhere to get high, wasting their opportunities in favour of talking about 'boners' and how some girl was 'gagging for it' based on what she was wearing that day. I can act laddish when need be, but I preferred to hang out with girls and a select few guys who were the 'arty' type. Whilst Dad didn't let me take art A-Level or music, it didn't stop me hanging out with those that did. My guitar playing was good enough that I joined a few of the talented musicians out on the field where we'd often jam in our break times.

"Have you seen the film *Jaws*?" Lucas asked, another dumb question.

"Yes, all of them, and yes, I have a phobia of sharks."

I always hated water-skiing with Dad; my legs would be dangling beneath me in the sea, waiting for the boat to pull me out of the water, and I couldn't get up fast enough. I would keep skiing for as long as I could, dreading the moment the rope would slacken and I would sink down into the dark inky water waiting for the boat to come back and pick me up. It felt like an eternity and I would hold my breath, imagining a shark lurking beneath me, attracted by the sound of the speedboat. My heart would not stop pounding until I was hauled back onboard.

"James!" My counsellor seems frustrated that my conversation is happening more in my head than with him.

"I've told you everything that happened that day, and there's nothing more I want to say." His probing really grates on me sometimes. It's like he enjoys poking a stick into an open wound.

"No, James, I was saying about the film *Jaws.*"

"What about it? I told you I've seen all of them."

"Well, do you remember the tagline from the film?"

"Huh? What tagline?"

"*Just when you thought it was safe to go back into the water.* It strikes me that each time you're doing well, each time you start to trust something or someone in life, another joke or prank is played on you. You never feel safe."

Chapter 26

RONNIE

The silence is deafening. I'm desperate for a cigarette but am nervous to break the silence as I don't want to agitate the big guy. His broad fingers clumsily sweep up the remains of Amanda's costume jewellery and throw it back in the jewellery box. The tangle of items is heaped in an untidy pile with the top layer stuffed on top and the lid wedged down.

"Stand up, Ronnie," he says matter-of-factly, his voice low and guttural. "It's time to get what I came for."

He beckons me to walk towards him, and I take a few tentative steps in his direction, wondering what on earth he wants from me this time.

The end of his shotgun is pointed directly at the centre of my forehead and I feel myself stiffen. His eyes are slightly bloodshot, and the black irises are like cold dark bullets.

The uncertainty of what is coming next is the worst fear I have ever experienced, my entire being clutching to its existence as if I'm hanging over the edge of a precipice, my fingers clawing at the rock and my feet trying to find their grip. I've never been a religious man; I don't believe in sitting in a church to confess your sins to be accepted through the Pearly Gates. Yet, I suddenly find myself praying. Begging for every wrong deed I have ever done consciously or unconsciously to be forgiven, and I pledge to make amends to every person I've ever wronged.

"I want the Cartier bracelet," he says.

It takes a second for the words to sink in. But then I snap into the present moment, my body convulsing as if I've just swallowed a large foreign object and it's trying to force its way down my windpipe. I feel a ripple snaking up my spine with goosebumps springing to the surface of every pore on my body.

"And don't tell me you sold it because I've checked. If you don't tell me where it is, your friends here will be cleaning up your blood from this beautiful cream carpet. Now wouldn't that be a waste of such a beautiful shag pile?"

Shit! No wonder he knew my name. It pieces together in a split second, and I know who my captor is. It's the big cocky guy, whose name evades me since I only met him the once, the mafia guy who I faced about eighteen months ago, at Jeremy's poker night. He suddenly materialises in my mind and I see the acne-scarred face that lies beneath the mask; the square jawline and thick straight hair that recedes at the forehead. I remember his blonde bimbo of a fiancée who had whispered in his ear, before removing the bracelet from her wrist and tossing it on the table to match my bet.

My brain rushes for an answer, something to say in response, but I'm stumped.

Checkmate.

I can't tell him what happened to the bracelet without my family learning that I've been having an affair. This is all my fault; he's here because of me. And I've dug a hole so deep I don't think I can ever get out of it.

My eyes glance to the side where I can see Amanda staring at me in confusion. Her innocence in all this makes me feel sick to the pit of my stomach. She has no idea what Big Guy has just asked me for, and I don't want her hearing my attempts at an explanation.

"Er, okay." I stall for time as I try to think how to handle this. If I say I haven't got it, he may shoot me here and now, in front of everyone, in front of my wife and son. I can't let that happen. Then it comes to me.

"You haven't asked about the safe," I say, in a lowered tone.

Yes, I need to get him out of this room, and away from prying eyes. "It's in the safe," I lie, my words barely audible so that they don't reach Amanda's ears.

"Then best you take me to this safe," he says, with a mocking edge to his tone, which hints that his patience is running thin.

As I turn to leave the room, Amanda signals her confusion, her head visibly shaking from side to side in bewilderment. I look at James, whose eyebrows are fixed

231

in a V-shape; his face is contorted as if he's in pain, and his eyes are glazed over as if he's high on drugs or something.

As we file out of the room in silence, I'm overwhelmed with heaviness. Will I be returning? Is this whole escapade about to end, without me getting the chance to ever hug my wife and son again? I leave them behind, uncertain of what lies in store, but praying they're kept safe.

We walk down the brightly-lit corridor towards my office; my chest is tight and my breathing laboured. What can I say to him? How is he going to react when he discovers there is no Cartier bracelet in the safe? It dawns on me that I would rather sacrifice my life than my family discover about the Cartier Panthère and my infidelity. I'm terrified of death, or at least, I'm frightened of nothingness. But the disclosure of my infidelity scares me even more.

I turn towards the office door. The lamp is still on in my office, which now feels like an empty tomb. The dark walls are claustrophobic and the air stifled in its tight space. I see a packet of Marlboro sitting on my desk next to the marble ashtray. I need to stall things.

"Please," I say, sounding pathetic, "can I have a cigarette? Shall we have a smoke?"

I know he smokes, well at least he did that night we played poker. I remember how his heavy gorilla hands seemed out of proportion, holding his cigarette that night. It had looked like a cocktail stick as he held it between two of his great thick fingers before putting it to his lips and then sucking on it like it was his last. But then I also recall him smoking a cigar, thinking the cigar was the same thickness as his fingers... or am I imagining that?

"Would you like a cigar?" I ask, prepared to get one from the sideboard.

"Where's the safe?"

"It's not there," I say, as he removes the family portrait from the wall in front of me.

I manoeuvre myself behind the desk to sit on my leather chair, putting some distance between us. My hands reach for the packet of cigarettes on the desk, and there's no objection, so I light the end of the cigarette, trying to keep my hands steady and not show my nerves.

His eyes take in the smooth panelled wall behind the portrait of James, Amanda and me, which he places on the floor, leaning it against the wall. He then scans the remaining walls for signs of a hidden safe. He seems unnerved by my calmness, but I've got nothing to lose and need to put on the performance of a lifetime if I'm to convince him that I'm being genuine. I intend to keep him away from the others, so they're kept in the dark about the Cartier bracelet, but I also need to somehow make sure that, whether he kills me or not, he leaves this place and keeps my secret.

"Why don't you take the balaclava off?" I ask, but he laughs.

"Look, I don't have it anymore—"

"I don't believe you. I know you would have taken it to Emcy's and my sources tell me that they haven't received a Cartier Panthère bracelet for resale. They did discover, however, that one was taken in for a valuation which perfectly fits the description of my wife's bracelet. No doubt you will realise therefore, that I overpaid you."

I note he says 'wife', but am not about to congratulate him on their nuptials. No doubt he made a vow that he would take his revenge and reclaim her Cartier bracelet for her.

I take a drag on my cigarette, feeling the nicotine hit the spot and giving me an illusory moment of relief.

"Yes, I did take it in to get it valued. But I gave it away, as a gift," I say, looking him square on. His pale lips form a smirk. "I gave it to my girlfriend, but my family can't know about it. Please, I'll do anything, give you anything, but this must stay between us."

"How convenient," he says. "I've heard about your acting skills, but let's hope for your sake that you're lying, because if it's not in the safe you're about to open, it's goodnight Vienna for you."

I offer the cigarette packet to him. "Do you want one?" I ask, struck with the strangeness of the situation. Here I am offering him a cigarette like this is a rendezvous with an old pal that I'm about to have a drink with, while he's pointing a sawn-off shotgun at my face.

"No, I want you to tell me where the bloody safe is." I sense his escalating anger. "You pushed me into a fucking corner that night, and you humiliated my missus. I don't take kindly to people who make a fool of me and it's payback time." I flinch as he leans towards me, recalling my first impression of him that poker night and believing there was something 'mafia-like' about him.

"Now, be a good boy, and fetch me what I want." He straightens up. "Tell me where the fucking safe is, before I put a bullet through your head, and then go back and put a bullet through your wife and little boy's heads."

I scream inside, looking at the discarded portrait to soak up the memory of that day, in case it's the last time I see them. It was James's twenty-first birthday, and we hired a photographer to come to our home and take some family shots. This is the one Amanda liked the best. James had had his hair cut a few days before and looks so handsome dressed in a suit and tie – not his usual choice of attire. He has Amanda's eyes and he towers above her with one arm linked in hers and the other resting on Max as we stand on our front porch. I'm on the edge of them both, beaming with pride, but I notice something I've never noticed before. Why didn't I put an arm around James? Why didn't I lean in the way Amanda is, showing such tenderness and pride both outwardly and inwardly? She seems to somehow look at the camera but has her head tilted in such a way that she's also looking at James, a proud smile on her face. I'm standing on the edge of them both like I don't really belong there; two's company, three's a crowd, as they say.

"Safe!"

"There's a hidden panel behind that picture," I say, pointing towards the vintage portrait of Fred Perry who is mid-point on Wimbledon Centre Court. It's framed in beautiful mahogany wood and was a gift from Amanda on my fortieth birthday.

My cigarette is burning quickly. I take another drag, inhaling deeply. This could be my final cigarette, and I'm going to make damn sure I get every last bit of it.

"Look, you can take it all," I say nervously. "I've got a couple of grand in cash in the safe, and I can write you a cheque for more."

I pick up my keys that are lying on the edge of the desk. "You can take the Aston," I say, offering them to him.

He looks at me quizzically before replying. "That's no use to me. I'm not going to get very far with it, am I?" He laughs, and the vision of his ugly face clearly appears through the thick fog of cigar smoke that he blew in my face that night.

And that's when it registers.

This guy isn't going to get very far with whatever he takes, even with the Cartier, had it been in my possession. It would be easy to track him down if I write him a cheque; he won't be able to cash it without being seized by the police. But, whatever he takes, he knows I know who he is now. I'm the only one who knows his identity, which can only mean one thing.

He intends to kill me.

Chapter 27

JAMES

The distant sound of a dog barking tugs at my heart. It's Max. He's here to rescue me. There are eyes burning into me. I sense them watching, forcing me to look up. I slowly lift my eyes to see everyone seated around me in the lounge. It must be Christmas; why else would everyone be gathered like this? But where's Grandma?

Ray and Lorraine are sitting at the end of the sofa, glaring at me, and Martyn and Meghan are looking at Mum who is also looking at me, with an expression I've never seen on her face before. Rachel is sitting next to Mum and she's crying. Why is she crying? Have I done something to upset her? What did I do?

I feel myself slowly waking up as if coming out of a dream, but something is wrong. Why isn't Rachel comforting me, telling me I've just had a bad dream? Why isn't Max here? He always lies with us when we have guests round, hoping for a few titbits or nibbles to fall on the floor.

The fog around me clears, and I look to the left side of me, where I see something black. I turn my head to get a better look and am greeted with the vision of someone dressed in black, like some sort of ninja. What the heck is Dad doing with a balaclava on? I know we get a bit engrossed in Christmas charades, but he's taking it a bit far, as per usual. He's even holding a replica pistol in some attempt to act out his charade, competitive as always to be the best.

"Batman." I hear the words fall as if they come from somewhere outside of me.

Rachel looks at me and I meet her glare. She looks confused, her eyes are wide and the look on her face is scaring me. What the hell did I just say?

I feel a tingle up my spine as the room becomes clearer. This is not a family Christmas scene. There are no decorations hanging from the ceiling or a tree proudly standing over in the far corner of the room.

Mum looks haggard and drawn; she has her arm around Rachel who is puffy-eyed and shivering. Why is she cold? Meghan and Martyn have their heads bowed as if they're praying whilst perched on the edge of their seats, and Lorraine is glaring at me, her eyes signalling some sort of warning. Ray is nervously tapping his knee, and…

But where's Daisy? I mean Max?

Holy shit!

It all comes flooding back to me. We were in a restaurant, eating pizza; Dad forgot the tickets and I drove them all back here. We were late for something. I

239

can't seem to recall what exactly, but we had to rush back here for something. Why are there so many blank spots?

I spot the gifts scattered all over the bar, then the 'Happy Birthday' sign hanging over the fireplace. This is no Christmas scene, there is no Max. It's Mum's birthday.

The person in black moves towards me,

"What did you say?" he asks. It's clearly not Dad, looking at his physique; Dad is far stockier than this man waving a silver thing under my nose.

"He said Batman," Mum says as if apologising for me. "You look a bit like Batman in that outfit, only I don't think Batman has a gun."

Oh God! I'm so stupid. Batman didn't have a gun; I've seen all the films and he never once uses a firearm. But shit, that's not how it was in the comics I read as a child; he *did* have a gun in those. I can clearly see him in his grey and blue body suit, with a black mask, pointing a silver pistol at the Joker. My brain is fizzing over again.

I try to speak, but the words won't come out of my mouth. I look at Rachel for reassurance, but it's as though her mute button has also been pressed. I stare at her, trying to tell her I'm sorry. I'm sorry that she met me, that I brought her into this crazy family. I'm sorry that I'm failing her, that I'm not the person she thought I was. Not the *man* she thought I was. I should be the one hugging her, telling her that everything is alright, but she's in Mum's arms, crying again. Dad has gone too far this time.

"Ssh, it's not good for the baby," Mum says. "Try and keep calm, sweetheart."

Baby? Oh Christ, we're having a baby. She's pregnant with my child and I let the secret out of the bag. Or did I? Is that why she's upset? I notice the handcuffs on her wrists and feel a rage rising up inside of me.

I raise my hands up to my head and push them through my hair, tugging at the roots, trying to wake myself out of this nightmare. The gun is waving precariously close to my left elbow. I grip my hair so tightly that I can feel it pulling my scalp, and then I release, throwing my arm against the black glove that's holding the silver pistol, knocking it out of his grip. It crashes onto the glass table in front of me, right on the spot where my Rolex watch had been just a short while ago.

Chapter 28

RONNIE

The smoke from my cigarette has nowhere to escape and it fills the corners of the room.

"Open it," Big Guy says, staring at the round metal dial on the safe door which was behind the hidden wall panel. I take a deep breath as I stub out my cigarette and his name comes to me in a flash of inspiration.

"Look, Pete. Is that your name? Pete?"

It occurs to me that I've watched some programme or read some article about hijack situations where I learnt that it's harder for your abductor to harm or kill you if you make yourself more 'human'; establish rapport.

"Why don't you take the balaclava off, you must be boiling underneath there."

He turns towards me and points the gun directly at my face. "Open the safe," he says, ignoring my words.

"Is that thing loaded?" I ask, staring straight down the barrel as he points it at me.

"What do you think? I suggest you open this damn safe before you find out."

I reluctantly rise from my chair and manoeuvre around the desk to join him by the safe, which is waiting for me at chest level. I notice, standing so close to him, that he's a full head taller than me. I look up at him, and make eye contact.

"Look, I've told you I don't have it, but I can get it for you next week."

I'll have to explain to Penny, which probably won't go down too well if I've just told her that I'm ending things. But if I arrange to see her one more time before ending it, perhaps I could say that I need to take the bracelet for insurance purposes or something. My brain is foggy; nothing is making sense. If I do that, there'll be a police search out on these guys, and I'll be accused of collaborating with them.

I need to make him trust me, reach some sort of a deal to make him believe that I'll get him the bracelet, but what assurance can I give him?

"Look, I gave it to my girlfriend," I say, but he interrupts me before I can continue.

"Do I have to count down from ten?" he says, taking a step back to let me position myself in front of the safe.

This is not working, and my heart starts racing. How can I make him listen to me?

I reach my hand towards the dial and pause, panicking at what may be about to happen when he learns that the bracelet isn't inside. With each move of the dial, I feel as though my time is up on death row and the guards are walking me the long mile towards my demise. I pray for that one last chance; that last-minute phone call that tells the world I'm innocent, before they strap me into the chair.

"I haven't got all day." His gravelly voice catches in his throat and he coughs, spraying the room with saliva that I feel on the back of my neck.

I ease the dial a quarter of a rotation to its final marker and hold my breath as I hear the click. There's a wad of notes waiting inside, which I'm more than happy to surrender, plus Amanda's Rolex that is worth a fair whack and that I'm equally happy to hand over. I pray that it will be a suitable consolation prize when this brute of a man realises there's no Cartier bracelet.

I reach my hand inside, and feel the wad of notes against my fingers, but before I've retracted my hand my senses are jolted.

"Put the gun down."

The voice doesn't belong to Pete, but neither does it belong to Sean, whom we left in the lounge. I freeze on the spot, my arm still inside the safe as I hear the hammer being pulled back to cock the gun.

Chapter 29

RONNIE

Pete's heavy shotgun clatters to the ground, and I turn to be greeted by the formidable sight of something I could never have imagined. While Pete is standing in front of me with his arms raised above his head, James is standing by the office door, pointing a silver revolver.

My brain cannot register what is happening.

He must have overthrown Sean somehow, and either the man is now cuffed to a table with another pair of handcuffs, or he's made a hasty exit. I'm guessing the police must be on their way, as James would have known to instantly press the panic button for help.

I shove Pete to the side, giving me a clear view of James, and for reasons I cannot decipher, I put my hand across Pete as if to protect him.

"It's time we put an end to all this," James says, with an unnervingly cool tone to his voice. But as I take in the scene in front of me, I'm jolted by the realisation that my son is standing before me with a loaded gun. Worse still, is the slow awakening that the gun is pointed at me, not at Pete.

Why the heck is he pointing it in my direction?

"James, put it down," I say, dropping the money and reaching forwards. My heart is pulsing in my ears. I feel the sweat surface on the back of my neck. What is he doing?

"Why?" he replies, in an almost mocking voice.

Is he on some power trip? I wonder. *Has he singlehandedly disarmed Sean only to become some kind of hero?* And then with his next sentence my whole world comes crashing down on me.

"It's only got fucking Blu Tack pellets in." The words are half-sung, half-shouted, and then he lets out a manic laugh.

"Or is it a replica?" he says, a glazed look reappearing in his eyes.

Christ!

He thinks I'm behind this. He bloody well thinks I've set this whole thing up and that the gun isn't real, like that time when I loaded the air rifle with pellets made from Blu Tack. Technically, that wouldn't be possible with the gun he's holding, but he doesn't know that. He's lost the plot.

I take a step towards him. Pete is visibly shaking and takes cover behind me which I'm happy for him to do; I can't let James fire that thing, if he harms anybody, it will destroy him, whether it's self-defence or not. I cannot stand and watch my own son shoot someone down in cold blood and suffer consequences that he doesn't deserve.

"James, it's not Blu–"

A thunderous crack fills the room and then there is darkness.

A pulsating noise resonates in my head, and all I can see is red, but from where, I cannot fathom. There's a crushing pain and I'm disorientated, trying to both breathe and not breathe. My body fizzes with electricity and there's a warmth in my chest.

I can vaguely hear something in the distance. It sounds like sirens. The muffled wails are fading in and out, as if someone is turning the volume switch up and down on the stereo.

There's the sound of running, then voices shouting – at me. Someone's calling my name, over and over.

My ears are ringing with silence as if my head is underwater, my whole being now shivering and it's cold, so cold.

I'm overwhelmed with exhaustion, like nothing I've ever experienced.

Red swirls flourish before my eyes, before they slowly begin to darken. I'm engulfed with calm as a kaleidoscope of dark browns and greens slowly pull me into a tunnel where my heaviness finally starts to lift.

Everything goes black.

Chapter 30

AMANDA

I slide my foot into the tip of the stocking. Ronnie loved stockings and today of all days, I want to give him the best. The clips are fiddly and I feel the bulk of the suspenders under my black dress. I reach for the black velvet jacket at the back of my wardrobe which will keep off any chill, and I choose a moderately high-heeled pair of black court shoes. I usually go for comfort over glamour, but Ronnie loved it when I put high heels on, and I find myself wishing I had worn them more often.

The reflection in the full-length mirror is not me. I don't even like black, let alone stockings and suspenders. I don't *do* heels. I don't *do* dresses. I don't *do* being a widow.

It's been three weeks since we lost him; there was a delay with the post-mortem, and due to the investigation we weren't permitted to bury him until now. Lorraine took care of all the details; I've been too busy consoling Rachel and finding professional help for James. He's currently sectioned at The Priory clinic, deeply traumatised by the whole event. The doctors say he's doing okay; he's beginning to understand that he's not responsible for his father's death. His brain was triggered, and he believed he was a child again with Ronnie playing a prank on him. He believed the gun was a fake.

I knew James had left us by the glazed expression on his face, confirmed by the mumbling that was incoherent until he suddenly shouted 'Batman,' as if we were all playing a game of charades. It was clear by the bewilderment in his eyes and his reluctance to look at me, that he was in some sort of shock. But nobody expected what happened next.

Once he picked up the gun from the coffee table he tore out of the lounge like a whirlwind. It all happened so fast. The burglar picked up his holdall and escaped through the patio doors and, after locking them, I ran to the kitchen to press the panic button. And then I heard the gunshot.

The solicitors say that we have nothing to worry about; James won't be charged with manslaughter, and we may not even have to attend court since we have all given individual statements of what happened that night, as well as details of all the pranks that Ronnie played in the past. The police reckon the armed robbers were amateurs, that they were using us as a practice run for something bigger that they had planned.

But why us?

I keep going over that question in my head. I've gone through the whole evening with a fine-toothed comb, reliving it with Meg and Martyn, Lorraine and Ray, but none of us understand. Why pick on our house that night when there are a multitude of bigger and better properties than ours around here?

The guilt is overwhelming. Thoughts keep getting stuck in a repeat loop in my head. What if I had been braver and reached for the panic button in the kitchen when I was taken to let the dogs out? What if I had rushed to find James first, rather than heading for the panic button in the kitchen? I might have been able to stop him.

The psychiatric report says that James believed the guns were fake. He experienced some sort of psychotic episode where he relived his childhood experience when Ronnie shot him with Blu Tack from an air rifle. He was unable to gauge the reality of the situation and believed that Ronnie had set up one of his pranks, which makes things even more horrific.

I pray at night that with psychiatric support, James will come through this. I've lost my husband, and I don't want to lose my son as well.

"Amanda?"

Rachel enters my bedroom. She's wearing a black trouser suit with a dark green silk blouse; her stomach is slightly rounded, but only I would notice this, knowing her as I do. Her hair is beautiful, knotted in a low chignon with a few strands cascading to her shoulders. But there's no makeup. Not today. Her eyes are red around the rim and the dark half-moons under her eyes show the exhaustion she's suffering.

"I'm off to collect James, we'll be back in an hour or so. Your mum is downstairs making you a cup of tea; will you be alright?" she says.

"Yes, sweetheart, tell Mum I'll be down in a bit. Drive carefully and I'll see you both in an hour."

She's been amazing through this whole nightmare. Always calm in a crisis, but no doubt feet paddling frantically under the water. God, I love her. She's like a daughter to me; the daughter I never had. She and James haven't even taken their vows yet, but 'in sickness and in health' is already in motion and she takes it all in her stride.

James couldn't speak after the event and was almost catatonic from the moment he saw his father die in front of him. I wish I could take it all away, tell him that the whole thing *was* some elaborate hoax, but sadly it wasn't. The nightmare was real, and one that is going to haunt his mind forever – as it will all of us.

Rachel tells me she blames herself. She says that she wishes she had tried to encourage him sooner to find some counselling for his dark moods, but I keep telling her, it would have made no difference. He's getting the right care now, and that's all that matters.

James has started to function again now the drugs are kicking in. He's able to dress himself, carry out a few daily activities and is eating again. He's developed a pitiful stutter which the doctors assure us will pass with

251

time, and he's signed off work for three months to give him enough time to recover fully.

Rachel and James are coming to stay here when he gets out of hospital, so that we can all be together, and I can support Rachel with James's recovery. Of course, I worry about her too. The stress of all this could be damaging for the baby, but she's fourteen weeks now and the doctors say that everything is fine, and they'll keep a close eye on her. I have insisted on sending her private; she deserves the best possible care to give this baby the best chance, and it's the least I can do.

I wipe yet more tears from my cheeks as I think about the grandchild that will be here in another seven months. Ronnie was so excited at the thought of being a grandfather one day; no doubt he would have spoilt them to the hilt, but that's my job now. I will be the best grandmother to this child and love it as if it were my own, without intruding on Rachel of course – she must come first and I'm aware that her own mother needs to take priority, meaning I must take a back seat when required. But the baby gives us all hope, the one good thing to come out of this whole damn mess.

I sit at my dressing table and switch the lamp on. As I brush my hair, I make the decision to wear it loose; Ronnie preferred it when I wore my hair down, and whilst I again regret my indifference to his requests, I push it from my mind. He'll be watching, from somewhere, I'm convinced of that. He'll be proud to see me – the glamorous widow, stoic and strong, the new head of our family unit.

After dabbing my cheeks with a tissue, I put a tinted moisturiser on my face before adding some powder and a touch of colour to my cheeks. If I end up streaking, then so be it, but I'm wearing makeup for my Ronnie today.

They say grief has different stages. I have no idea what stage I'm in, but I'm riddled with regrets. There are so many what ifs. So many if onlys. If only I had spent a little less time down at the stables and been around him more. If only we had spent more time doing things together rather than going our separate ways. But I'm not into tennis, business, or fast cars, all of which were his passions in life.

We slowly reached a sort of understanding, allowing each other to pursue our individual interests during the day, but then coming together for dinner in the evenings with a glass of Merlot and conversation about what we'd been up to. We were creatures of habit, and, if I'm honest, Ronnie wasn't the easiest person to be around. He was a 'jump' kind of man; he expected you to jump to his command, and when you did, he would ask you to jump higher. He was selfish too. There was never any joint decision making, it was always his way, or no way. But I needed him, in the same way that he needed me.

I lost my confidence (if I ever had any in the first place) after having James. Ronnie stood by me when I was quite literally terrified. He held my hand and reassured me that everything would be alright and gave me confidence to become the mother that I am. I've never been driven or career-minded like him, and he's provided the safety net that I needed to stay at home and look after my family – and my horses.

I feel guilty when I think how much time I have dedicated to my horses in recent years, but when empty nest syndrome kicked in and Ronnie continued to spend increasing amounts of time away with business deals or tennis tournaments, it gave me a purpose. It gives me a purpose today. I have a deep connection with horses, always have done. They are peaceful, gentle creatures who are naturally calming and relaxing – you could say they are my therapy.

The super king-size bed seems excessively big now. As I smooth down the top throw and position the cushions, I think about how I wish Ronnie and I had made love more recently. It bothered him that my sex drive was lower than his, but frankly, I'd rather have a cup of tea than that whole messy business. I told him once to go and take a lover, when he was pawing me through my silk pyjamas, practically pleading with me to succumb. I didn't mean it of course; I wouldn't want anything, or anyone, to threaten our family unit and what we've built, and I know he was always loyal. But now, I'd give anything for him to be here; my body physically aches for him when I lie in our bed at night. There's a huge void when I stretch my limbs out, the place where our legs would rub, or, if I took up too much space, would be nudged back to my side of the bed. I crave his body, to feel his skin against mine, to smell the familiar smell of his aftershave. God, I miss him.

The doctor has given me some tranquilisers. I'm not one for taking medication, but when I get flashbacks of that evening, crouching down and pressing my hands into all the blood on his chest, trying to stem the flow, I need something to stop my heart pounding as if I were there again. I need something to numb the feeling of holding Ronnie in my arms and crying into his face, kissing him and begging him to please open his eyes. The paramedics tore him away from me, carrying out emergency procedures whilst we stood in the corridor stricken with horror, shortly followed by grief when they told us he was gone.

It feels like a warped version of some Aesop's fable, like the boy who cried wolf. Ronnie spent his life playing practical jokes on us all, like a child who just couldn't grow up, and we all made idle threats to get him back one day. But the truth is, our minds never worked as quickly as his, we never found the opportunity – that spur-of-the-moment decision where we could see the perfect joke to play back on him. And yet, the irony in all of this is that we all suspected at one moment or another that he may have been behind the hold-up that night, while he must have believed it was one of us. I still can't quite believe that Ronnie's practical jokes ended up being his own tragedy.

One consolation is that if Ronnie thought it was payback, that one of *us* had planned the hoax for him, he would have known it wasn't me. I was the only one who thought we were meant to be at the theatre and had no idea that everyone was coming back to ours, but Ray and James knew, as did all the guests at the party.

As I enter the kitchen, Mum places a cup of tea in front of me with a piece of toast. I can't eat, my stomach is a mass of knots.

"The caterers called," she says. "They'll be here at twelve to set everything up, you don't need to worry about a thing. Your sister's meeting us at the church." She gives me a knowing look, a look of pity.

We lost my dad nearly eight years ago now, and whilst the pain lives with her daily, Mum assures me that life grows around the pain. It never goes away, apparently, nor does it shrink, but rather fits into a new world which somehow continues to expand. Her eyes transmit that she knows what I'm going through, that somehow, even though I don't know it yet, I will come out the other side of this.

But Dad had cancer. We had known for some time that he was going to die, and being as he was eighty-one, some ten years older than Mum, there was always an expectation that he would go before her. But Ronnie? This feels like we have accidentally put a film on at the end, taking a sneaky preview before rewinding back to watch from the beginning. I so wish I could rewind.

Our time wasn't supposed to be over now, we had so much to do yet. We were going to travel, visit places around the world that neither of us had seen. We had a

256

joint bucket list that we often talked about, things we were saving. Ronnie always said he was going to write a book… perhaps one day I'll do that for him. Dedicate it to him in memory of the great man that he was.

I know his jokes were a little twisted at times, but he meant no real harm by them. I don't think he ever really thought through the consequences or considered how people might or might not react, but he went and did them anyway. He had an incredible mind, so creative and incredibly shrewd. He was well respected in the business world and it's thanks to him that I won't have to worry about money for the rest of my days.

They say money doesn't buy happiness, and it doesn't. I can't imagine ever feeling happy again. But it does bring peace of mind to know it's one less thing to worry about. It brings security and some comfort to know that I can afford to get through the rest of my life without money worries, ensuring James and his family are well looked after too. I'm the main shareholder in the business now, receiving Ronnie's annual dividend, and whilst I'm not able to directly get involved, or for that matter having any desire to, I know Martyn will ensure that everything is taken care of.

Ronnie leaves a great legacy behind – a multi-million-pound business that will provide for his family and friends. And memories too, both good and bad, of the fun character that he was. Yes, he was a practical joker, and no, he wasn't a saint. But he didn't deserve his life to be cut short before any of us were ready to say goodbye.

In my mind, he died a hero. He did everything he could that night to protect us all, and when he led the big guy out of the lounge, he was so calm; the expression on his face when he looked at me for the last time, was one of comfort and reassurance.

If only I'd had the chance to tell him how much I love him.

Chapter 31

JAMES

My head is full of so much anger. Anger that is filling me up like a tap I can't switch off. I understand what has happened, although I don't fully compute that it was *me* in the study that night. I don't remember pulling the trigger and shooting Dad; I don't remember anything from the point when Rachel came back into the room after being taken to the toilet by one of those masked bastards.

Rachel has had to go through the pain of filling in the gaps for me, since my brain seems to have frozen from the point where I was so angry that Dad was putting my wife and child through such an ordeal. It was like something inside me snapped and some other force took over. I still feel spaced out, although Mum says it's a side-effect of the drugs they've put me on.

The doctors are still in the process of finding a diagnosis for what's wrong with me. They've thrown around labels like PTSD, schizoaffective disorder, and psychosis. I don't want to think about it; I'm taking it one day at a time, and keeping the thought of Rachel and our baby in the forefront of my mind to drive me through my journey to recovery. I cannot give up; I know I need to get well, for them. Rachel needs me, and I need to sort my head out so that I can be there for her. It should be me supporting her, not the other way round.

The smell of leather seats and the lemon air freshener make me feel queasy. I ask Rachel to open the window slightly to let a little fresh air into the limousine. I'm aware of Mum and Rachel's hands locked in mine, but I can't feel them. I still feel numb inside and I'm struck by how they both seem like robots, programmed to help me get through today, and tell me that this is all over and everything is going to be okay now.

My eyes stay fixed straight ahead at the flowers that spell 'DAD' in the hearse in front. The white chrysanthemums are edged with red ribbon that looks like blood spilling out of the word, and the red rose detail at the edge of the first letter looks like a bullet wound full of congealed blood.

I grind my teeth.

My dad is gone, and I want revenge. Revenge for the fact that someone got to play their sick joke on him and my family, and they took it too far. Rachel says the police have no lead, nothing to go on yet, but it makes no sense. How can two masked gunmen just vanish into thin air, like magic? How can they get away with what they put us through that night and consequently the rest of our lives, without some sort of payback for their actions?

I watch Mum and Rachel as they cry through the ceremony, but my tears won't come. My psychiatrist says they will in time, but it's like I've forgotten how to cry. Perhaps they are frozen somewhere deep inside waiting to melt like some great glacier slowly thawing before it becomes a waterfall, but all I can think about is finding those guys. I won't believe Rachel and my child are safe until they are caught.

The CCTV cameras have been checked, I'm told, but I desperately want to watch the recordings myself. Apparently only the skinny guy was caught entering the house, but he had positioned himself at such an angle behind guests that you couldn't see his face. Nobody remembers seeing him either. Everyone from the party has been questioned but not a single person can recall seeing him or speaking to him when he walked straight through the front door of our house. It's like he was the invisible man, for Christ's sake, snaking his way in, unseen and unheard, his identity disguised in broad daylight.

The police think he went straight to the cloaks cupboard pretending to hang his jacket up and struck the jackpot when he found the switch for the internal cameras, since there is no recording of anything that happened from that point onwards. Then, they think he slipped into the downstairs toilet and waited for the right moment to slide off to the gym, opening the patio doors to let the other guy in and both hiding out while everyone enjoyed Mum's party. But if they were amateurs like the police reckon, then how come they haven't found a lead? Why haven't they found out how they knew about the party, or how they managed to slip away in the chaos of the shooting, leaving just as surreptitiously as they arrived?

I won't rest until they're found; my mind goes over and over it every second of the day, searching for the missing answers as if trying to mentally solve a Rubik's cube. My life cannot resume until those bastards are caught and pay their dues for their crime. There's also a part of me that, for some reason, cannot fully comprehend that this wasn't a prank, set up by someone. I've been told it wasn't, but my paranoia still believes that someone, somewhere, wanted their payback on Dad, and I need proof before I'll believe this wasn't all a hoax that went terribly wrong.

As the coffin is lowered, I hold Rachel as she weeps on my shoulder. I whisper goodbye to my dad, adding, *I'll find them, Dad, I promise.*

Then, the strangest sensation of calm comes over me as I watch the coffin finally disappear. Tension dissipates from my body, and my head clears as words fill my head. I don't know if the words are mine or if someone else's voice is echoing in my head but I feel shocked by them; they are words I will never repeat out loud.

You're safe now.

Chapter 32

AMANDA

The church service goes by in a blur. I take in how packed the pews are in the village church that doesn't feel much bigger than our lounge at home. I bow my head as I walk up the aisle, not wanting to acknowledge all the pitying looks that I can feel boring into me.

My eyes fixate on the altar at the front of the church, trying to keep them from wandering to the spot where my husband is lying, so close to me, and yet so far. The altar cloth is a white fabric with lines of gold, a large green panel bearing a silver embroidered cross draped in the centre.

Ray steps up to give his eulogy. He takes his place on the dark oak pulpit and I feel warm tears streaking my cheeks. I can't look at him; I accidentally caught his eye when he started, and we both nearly lost it. My eyes focus on the heavy oak canopy that is suspended above him by a black chain. Christ! Don't let another disaster happen. The thought of it crashing down on Ray crosses my mind and I realise just how much I need him now. We are connected by our love for Ronnie, but more than

263

that, he always took care of both of us as if we were family. He's like a brother to me – as he was to Ronnie.

Ray's words are perfect, but how do you sum up someone like Ronnie in a three-minute speech? Yes, he was driven, successful, the life and soul of a party and above all somebody that everybody had respect for. But he was my husband, and I knew the insecure little boy that needed to be loved, handled in the right way to avoid a tantrum, and ignored when he threw his toys out of the pram. I knew how he liked his toast browned but not burnt, with two teaspoons of my homemade marmalade and butter melted to a spreadable consistency. I knew when he needed his ego boosting with a few tender words, when he needed company, or when he needed space to work on yet another project in his office.

Ronnie never liked to talk about death, and I know it was his deepest fear, not knowing what was beyond this life. Another success for him now. Wherever we go, whatever there is beyond, he beat me to it. I guess I'm probably not alone in wishing I could tell him one more time that I love him. We would say it to each other every day, when we pecked each other on the cheek, but I want to tell him now that I really *do* love him, in the way we told each other in the early days, taking a moment to look directly into each other's eyes.

He was such a loyal and dependable man who loved our home as much as I do, and what came with it – our family, our life. And yet he never seemed satisfied, as though there was something he still needed to prove. He was always looking for the next challenge, something to fill that active mind of his. Well, he can finally switch off, take a rest now.

I spend the rest of the service fiddling with the clasp on the bracelet that Lorraine bought for me. It stirs the memory of how my beloved Tiffany bracelet was taken, with the charms that held so many fond memories: the 'Best Mum' charm from James on Mother's Day, the cute little paw print when we got Max, to name but two. I'm one for appreciating the sentimental worth of things as opposed to the monetary value; I keep everything, from the first cinema ticket when Ronnie and I were dating, to a restored horseshoe from the first horse I ever fell in love with when I was just twelve, all of them safe in a box on the top shelf of my wardrobe. I feel a pang of grief as I rub the silver bangle, imagining the possible future charms that have been taken from me… just like my future memories with Ronnie. And then it dawns on me…

The burglar asked Ronnie something about a bracelet just before he led him off to the office. He said something about a Cartier bracelet, and I have clean forgotten until this moment. I make a mental note to mention this to the police, since, whilst I know we don't possess any pieces by Cartier, it may have some relevance. I'm not sure if anyone else picked up on it, but in discussions that we've had, nobody else has mentioned it.

We file out of the church, following the large mahogany casket, the roses that Lorraine ordered for me balanced on the lid. The music is playing one of Ronnie's favourite tracks, and it feels like his last prank on me. He wrote in his will that he wanted 'Going Underground' by the Jam and I sense the awkwardness of the congregation as we shuffle out to such an inappropriate, upbeat track. It is helping to keep me together though, so thank you, my darling, for that.

As I stand around outside to say goodbye and thank the people who are setting off back to our house, I fix a fake smile on my face. It feels unnatural, but what else can I do? I guess you could call it my poker face, which I don't think is half as convincing as Ronnie's. But I'm dreading what comes next, and only people who knew him well are coming to the burial.

I'm so grateful the sun is shining; even the golden reflection on the path that leads out of the church seems to be glowing, as if Ronnie has planned the perfect weather for his special occasion.

I'm greeted with kisses and hugs from all sides, with Mum and Emma staunchly standing either side of me, giving silent support. Barbara, Ronnie's mother, comes up to join us. I've always found her a cold character, and we've never been close. I don't think Ronnie was particularly close to her either; he resented her for sending him away to boarding school. She appears so much older than when I last saw her, which was nearly a year ago now. The black net that covers her face fails to hide the haunted look of bewilderment. She is clearly fragile, and I fear that if Ronnie's sister, Sandra, lets go of her, she will collapse to the floor and need to be scooped up like a broken bird to be carefully guarded in a box until her wings are mended. Whilst I'm not particularly fond of her, she is the hardest one for me to keep up my poise with because she's a mother; I cannot dwell on how it would feel to lose my precious son, and I thank God that James is still here, even if he is a little broken too.

Rachel grabs my arm and guides me around the back of the church with James where we are to say our final farewells to my dear husband, the man who has stood by my and James's side and provided for us for the last twenty-three years. The man who, despite his childish ways, was loyal, faithful, and honourable to the end.

Lorraine steps forwards and hugs me as I start to cry by the graveside. Rachel and James are in each other's arms, and she is sobbing into James's shoulder as the coffin is slowly lowered into the grave.

Despite the sunshine, I suddenly feel cold from head to toe. Lorraine hands me a red rose, and I step forward onto the cushion of soft grass by the edge of the muddy mound. Silent tears fall as I stand and watch my husband lowered into his final home.

My red rose lands on top of the coffin and I whisper my final goodbye before being grabbed by Lorraine who pulls me back as I become overwhelmed with grief. She holds me tightly as I weep, looking down at the dark wooden box, wishing that he would spring out of it and tell me this is all just an elaborate hoax.

For Christ's sake, Ronnie, come back, tell us this is all going to be over, make me feel safe again.

Lorraine stays with me a while as everyone pays their respects, nodding their heads as they look at the coffin before making their way to shake my hand or peck me on the cheek. She leaves me to have my final moment alone with Ronnie.

As the space around me clears, I notice a woman in a short black dress, her heels half-sunk in the grass, reluctant to join the others who are leaving. There's something familiar about her, but I don't recall where or even *if* I've seen her before.

As she finally makes to leave, I walk across and stop her; she's not family and it seems odd that a stranger would be standing by my husband's graveside.

"Hello. Sorry, have we met?" I say as I approach her.

There's something about her dark glossy mane that gives me a feeling of déjà vu, but what is she doing here, standing by herself?

She turns and looks at me. Her stunning green eyes looking directly into mine.

"Oh, I was a friend of Ronnie's," she says, with some hesitation in her voice. "We worked together."

I notice her perfectly-applied lipstick edged with lip liner and makeup that hasn't shifted an inch with any tears.

"I'm his wife, Amanda," I say, stretching my hand forwards to greet her.

She smiles nervously and responds by reaching her hand out, the sleeve of her black jacket retreating slightly as she places her perfectly manicured hand into mine.

And that's when I see it.

Coiled round her wrist is a diamond and onyx bracelet, a panther head glaring at me with emerald eyes. I may not be a woman with expensive tastes, but I know what this is – it would be hard not to. It's a Cartier bracelet.

A Panthère de Cartier, I think it's called.

Acknowledgements

Martin Rodwell. First and foremost to my beloved husband Martin for always encouraging me when I'm riddled with doubts. Thank you for tirelessly listening to me read chapters out aloud and believing in me more than I believe in myself. I wouldn't be where I am today and I wouldn't have published *The Hoax* if it weren't for your loving support.

Alison Williams – editor. Thank you for the initial beta read and your encouraging comments that motivated me to continue with this book.

The edits that followed helped to improve my writing, and, with your expert guidance and suggestions, the book was shaped into what it has become today.

This is the third book we have worked on together, and I hope our relationship will continue as I write further books. It would be true to say that I would not have continued writing if it were not for your inspirational support and ability to bring out the best in me and my writing. Your reports are always detailed, well-balanced and sensitive. I hit the jackpot finding you!

Julia Gibbs – proofreader. I'm so glad to have met you both as a friend, and as someone who introduced me to the writing community. Your knowledge of and talent with grammar is outstanding – if not a little weird at times! I'm grateful to have my book proofread in your safe hands.

Georgia Rose – formatter. A wonderful author and writing friend who has been a great influence during my early writing years. Thank you for taking on the task of formatting this book.

Advanced Readers. Thank you to the women from 'North Norfolk Bookworms' who offered their support by reading *The Hoax* before publishing. Your comments and feedback have been invaluable.

Can You Help?

Thank You For Reading My Book!

I really appreciate all of your feedback, and I love hearing what you have to say. If you are able to, please leave me an honest review on Amazon letting me know what you thought of the book. Or you can just leave a star rating if you prefer. You might not think your opinion matters, but I can assure you it does. It helps the book to gain visibility and helps other readers to decide whether to purchase it or not, so if you could take a minute or two it would be much appreciated. If you have a paperback in your hand and think 'this request doesn't include me', please think again. It doesn't matter how or where you bought your paperback, Amazon, Goodreads and BookBub will still accept a review from you.

Thank you

Nikki

Free Exclusive Content:

Thank you so much for sharing my journey by reading *The Hoax*. I love to interact with my readers and would like to continue sharing my journey with you via my newsletter. If you sign up to that here https://bit.ly/the-hoax. I will send you some exclusive content, only available to my subscribers, for free.

About The Author

Nikki Rodwell is the author of Amazon best-seller memoir *Catch Me if I Fall*. She has also published a debut collection of poetry called *A Mother's Lament*, before finding her niche in fiction.

Nikki's passion in both reading and television is psychological and domestic thrillers, which led to her debut thriller *The Hoax*. She is currently working on her next thriller novel, to be released later this year.

When not writing, Nikki enjoys a quiet life in North Norfolk with her husband Martin and their two dogs, Chester and Mabel. They own a café in a seaside town and enjoy walking on beaches and in the surrounding North Norfolk countryside.

To find out more or to book her for speaking events, please visit:

Website – **www.nikkirodwell.co.uk**

FB /nikkirodwellauthor
Instagram @nikkirodwellauthor
Twitter @nikkirodwell

Other Books by Nikki Rodwell

Catch Me if I Fall – how mental health broke my back but didn't break me.

A Mother's Lament – A short collection of poetry.

Printed in Great Britain
by Amazon